Appleby Talks About Crime

Appleby Talks About Crime

by **Michael Innes**

Edited by John Cooper

Afterword by Dr. Margaret Macintosh Harrison

Crippen & Landru Publishers
Norfolk, Virginia
2010

ISBN (clothbound edition): 978-1-932009-91-0

ISBN (trade softcover edition): 978-1-932009-92-7

FIRST EDITION

Printed in the United States of America

Crippen & Landru Publishers
P. O. Box 9315
Norfolk, VA 23505
USA

Email: info@crippenlandru.com
Web: www.crippenlandru.com

CONTENTS

INTRODUCTION

JOHN INNES MACKINTOSH STEWART (1906–1994) wrote novels and short stories under his own name but used the pseudonym Michael Innes for his more popular crime fiction, mostly featuring Scotland Yard Inspector (later Superintendent, later Commissioner) John Appleby.

Stewart came from a refined background and was educated at Edinburgh Academy. He states in his autobiography *Myself and Michael Innes* (1987):

> My memories of my schooldays are scanty and unremarkable, yet they cover eleven years! On more than two thousand occasions, that is to say, I must have pushed my bicycle into those pebbled yards in the morning, and then out of them in the afternoon, whether homeward or to some playing-field. I don't doubt that in that long stretch there was plenty of fun as well as much boredom and a certain chronic apprehensiveness never amounting to anything like terror.

He goes on to write that whilst at the Academy, the school's headmaster had stated "that [he] might one day manage a *Coral Island* but that a *Treasure Island* would lie beyond the twitch of [his] tether."

In 1925, Stewart went up to Oriel College, Oxford where he took a First in English Language and Literature in 1928. In his autobiography, he writes that his friend, A.J.P. Taylor, "decided it would be perfectly reasonable to top off a university education with a kind of Grand Tour and [I] set off for Germany and Austria accordingly, accompanied by several other members of the unemployed class."

On returning to England in 1930, he took up a lectureship at Leeds University which he held until 1935. It was here he met Margaret Hardwick, whom he married in 1932. They were to have five children.

In 1935, John Stewart then became Jury Professor of English at Adelaide University in Australia, where he stayed until 1945; it was on the ship to Australia that he wrote his first detective novel. (An important part of the narrative in *Lament for a Maker* (1938) takes place in Australia.) In January 1946, he took up a lecture-ship at Queen's University, Belfast. Stewart probably drew on his own experience of Belfast and Northern Ireland for his novel *The Journeying Boy* (which is known as *The Case of the Journeying Boy* in the United States; both editions published in 1949). Incidentally, he thought this was the best of his work under the Innes name.

In June 1948, Stewart moved to Oxford and in 1949 he became a Student (Fellow) in English Literature at Christ Church, where he remained until 1973. For the last four years at Oxford, he was University Reader.

In *Myself and Michael Innes*, Stewart claims that in his later years at school and during his five years at Leeds, he read dozens of detective stories. These included books by Agatha Christie, of whose work he spoke highly, and Ellery Queen. He says, "Indeed, it was when the thought came to me that in something like the time I habitually spent reading detective stories I might well be able myself to write one that Michael Innes was, as it were, born."

Stewart has admitted that he was not a great creator of mystery plots. An image or line would come into his head. The crime and the mystery would then develop as he wrote, although he always knew what would be said on the last page. Most of his writing was done in the two hours before breakfast.

J. I. M. Stewart was a superlative writer and the books written as by Michael Innes have been variously described as witty, urbane, donnish, clever, erudite, charming, amusing and, most importantly, entertaining.

The *Times Literary Supplement* stated of the first Appleby novel, "It must be sufficient to indicate that *Death at the President's Lodging* is the most important contribution to detective litera-ture that has appeared for some time." It was published in the United Kingdom in 1936 but retitled for publication in the United States in 1937 as *Seven Suspects*. Gollancz, the British publisher, proudly proclaimed on the front of the yellow dust wrapper for the first edition, "This is the best 'first' Detective Story that has ever come our way."

Innes's first five novels all received good reviews and are considered to be classics in the history of crime fiction. *Hamlet, Revenge!* (1937) and *Lament for a Maker* make the lists of most people's favourites, although there are numerous treasures to be found in his later books. Some of his outstanding crime novels are *What Happened at Hazelwood* (1946), *Operation Pax* (United States title *The Paper Thunderbolt*, both editions 1951), *A Private View* (U.S. title *One Man Show*, both 1952), *The Long Farewell* (1958), *The New Sonia Wayward* (U.S. title *The Case of Sonia Wayward*, both 1960), *Silence Observed* (1961), *A Connoisseur's Case* (U.S. title *The Crabtree Affair*, both 1962), *The Bloody Wood* (1966) and *Honeybath's Haven* (U.K. 1977, U.S. 1978).

The author himself described his own detective stories as on the frontier between the detective story and the fantasy. In his autobiography, he admits that he has "always been reluctant to despatch [my] crooks and murderers to gaol or to the gallows, with the result that a high proportion of them meet with some form of poetic justice, are more or less ingeniously hoist with their own petard."

There is much quoting from literature in the books; extracts from Rudyard Kipling, Thomas Hardy, George Meredith, Robert Louis Stevenson, Samuel Coleridge and, of course, Shakespeare, all appear. With regard to Shakespeare, in *There Came Both Mist and Snow* (U.S. title *A Comedy of Terrors*, both 1940), the writer, Lucy Chigwidden, suggests a parlour game based on Shakespeare's bells. Amusingly, in *The Long Farewell*, the scholar Lewis Packford refers to Shakespeare as "Wally the Shake."

The novels contain many marvellous examples of Innes's ability to create imaginary scenes. Examples include the description of an industrial town in *There Came Both Mist and Snow* and that of the Stray at Harrogate in *The Daffodil Affair* (1942). The scene between Canon Rixon and Alice Packford, as the Canon administers pastoral care over a game of snakes and ladders (to be found in

The Long Farewell), is particularly well observed as is the wonderful description of a winter's journey through snow, first by train then by horse drawn carriage which starts *Appleby's End* (1945). These are just a few of my particular favourites.

Besides all the literary allusions, Innes had great fun with names for some of the villages and characters portrayed in his stories. Village names include Sneak, Boxer's Bottom, Deep Urchins, Snarl, Drool and Yatter. Servants at various establishments are Blight, Tarbox, Butt, Rainbird, Butter, Swindle and Litter. Fogg and Gale are solicitors whilst Rushout, Bultitude, Prisk and Prodger are all donnish individuals.

The forty-eight British first editions were all published by Victor Gollancz in boring uniform yellow dust wrappers which belie the entertainment these books contain for readers. Surely this is a classic example of the adage "Don't judge a book by its cover!"

John Stewart was a member of the Detection Club and wrote an Appleby story, "Pelly and Cullis," for their anthology *Verdict of Thirteen* (1979). The stories in that collection are linked by the fact that all of them concern a jury.

The quality of Innes's writing was recognised by several authorities. One of his skilfully plotted novels, *Lament for a Maker*, was listed in the "Haycraft-Queen Definitive Library of Detective-Crime-Mystery Fiction: Two Centuries of Cornerstones, 1748–1948." *Hamlet, Revenge!* was included by Julian Symons in *The Hundred Best Crime Stories* (1959). H. R. F. Keating recorded two novels, *Appleby's End* and *The New Sonia Wayward*, in his *Crime and Mystery, The 100 Best Books* (1987). In February 2008, Michael Innes was listed in the *Daily Telegraph* (London) article "50 Crime Writers to Read Before You Die."

John Stewart's first piece for radio (written like his other radio contributions under the pseudonym of Michael Innes) was "Strange Intelligence" featuring John Laurie. Broadcast on 30 June 1947, it dwells on an imaginary conversation at a real meeting on Saturday 21 August 1773 between Dr. Johnson, James Boswell and Lord Monboddo. John Laurie also featured in his second work, "The Hawk and the Handsaw," an item concerning Hamlet, and again produced by Rayner Heppenstall broadcast on 21 November 1948. He wrote around a dozen works for radio, mostly with a Shakespearean theme. The last to be broadcast was "The Bagpipes and the Bells" on 9 June 1961.

Only three examples of Innes's detective fiction have been adapted as radio plays. The first was the short story "The Heritage Portrait" adapted by Sam Hanna Bell and featuring Robert McLemon as Appleby. This was broadcast on 11 April 1961 but only on the Northern Ireland Home Service. Two novels were adapted for broadcast on BBC Radio 4: *Appleby's End* on 10 April 1982, with John Hurt as Appleby, and *Lament for a Maker* on 31 December 1988, with Michael MacKenzie as Appleby.

During 1964, 1968 and 1969, the British Broadcasting Corporation produced 45 episodes of a television series called *Detective*. Two of the episodes feature cases for John Appleby. On the 15 June 1964, an adaptation of the novel *A Connoisseur's Case* was shown, starring Dennis Price as Sir John Appleby and Ann Castle as Lady Judith Appleby. The short story "Lesson in Anatomy," in which Ian Ogilvy played Inspector Appleby, appeared on 7 June 1968.

In 1977, Walt Disney Productions loosely adapted Innes's *Christmas at Candleshoe* (1953) to produce the comedy-thriller *Candleshoe*. The film starred David Niven, Jodie Foster, Helen Hayes and Leo McKern. Compton Wyngates, a stately home in Warwickshire, England, posed as the fictional estate of Candleshoe.

It is as Michael Innes that John Stewart will mainly be remembered. His creation, Detective Inspector John Appleby, is purported to be named after a student whom Stewart taught at Leeds University. (That student went on to write crime fiction.) Appleby's first appearance in literature is his arrival at St. Anthony's College in a great yellow Bentley, "Scotland Yard's most resplendent vehicle." He is there to investigate the murder of Dr. Umpleby in *Death at the President's Lodging*. Shortly after his arrival, we are told "there was something more in Appleby than the intensely-taught product of a modern police college. A contemplative habit and a tentative mind, poise as well as force, reserve rather than wariness—these were the tokens perhaps of some underlying, more liberal education. It was a schooled but still free intelligence that was finally formidable in Appleby." In all Appleby appears in thirty-two novels and seventy-three stories. He came from quite an ordinary background (his grandfather was a baker) but showed promise at an early age by winning a county scholarship.

Appleby's favourite technique in his investigations is to sit back, watch and listen before coming to any conclusions. Every small detail must fit with the facts of the case. He is quite impressively educated with interests in literature, art, ballet and archaeology as well as being an intermittent angler. He likes amusing conversation and his speech is full of literary allusions and quotations. To him, police routine is not important but he is shrewd, persistent and like a "bloodhound unleashed." Although he is a successful detective and a confident person with the power to command, sometimes he thinks of himself as an "inglorious Sherlock Holmes." His superiors have great faith in his abilities. It is the Prime Minister himself who first briefs Appleby over the murder of the Lord Chancellor in *Hamlet Revenge!* and calls him their "Number One man."

Appleby smokes a pipe, cigarettes and cigars. In the early stages of his career, he is living in a humble flat in Westminster. He has two younger sisters, the elder, Patricia, is a manuscript expert working for the collector Jasper Shoon. In *Stop Press* (U.S. title *The Spider Strikes*, both 1939), her only book presence, she is asked by her friend Belinda what her brother is like. Her reply is "Distinctly superior. His clothes are made to measure … Five eleven and a half, fair hair and grey eyes, muscular and well-nourished." His younger sister, Jane, again with only one book appearance, is an undergraduate at Somerville College, Oxford. In *Operation Pax* (U.S., *The Paper Thunderbolt*) Jane finds real excitement amongst the book stacks of the Bodleian Library.

Appleby makes a sudden and surprising entry to the story *Appleby on Ararat* (1941). It is in this novel, whilst musing on how Sir Ponto Unumunu was killed, that he recaps his first five cases. He reminisces, "This was not the way to solve a mystery. It was not thus that he had plumbed the matter of Dr. Umpleby and the bones, of the stylish homicides at Scamnum Court, of the daft laird of Erchany; it was not thus that he had exposed the Friends of the Venerable Bede or preserved ten persons from the blackest suspicion by recollecting a line in 'The Ancient Mariner'." Later in this tale involving fantastical situations, Diana Kittery comments to Appleby, " 'love the way you talk … the way your mind goes. It's like watching Don Bradman bat.' He was startled at the enormousness of the compliment."

Appleby has a dictatorial aunt living in Harrogate who features in *The Daffodil Affair*. While on the Stray pondering the case, Appleby is spotted by his aunt and "his heart sinks." The Assistant Commissioner at The Yard had sent Appleby to Harrogate to look for Daffodil, a half-witted carriage horse, who has been stolen. This leads to another whimsical yarn. Even Superintendent Hudspith, one of the main characters in this book, says, " 'We're in a sort of hodge-podge of fantasy and harum-scarum adventure that isn't a proper detective story at all. We might be by Michael Innes.'

" 'Innes? I've never heard of him,' Appleby spoke with decided exasperation."

It is whilst on the train journey to Snarl in *Appleby's End* (1945) that he first meets the sculptress, Judith Raven, his future wife. "She had long haunches and slender flanks—she was, in fact, what old fashioned writers would call tall and slim—and she had long eyelashes and what it was possible to think of as a long nose. Her manner was severe—and composed." It doesn't sound promising! Later, when they decide to marry, she tells Appleby, "I'm marrying you for your wits." This sudden engagement in *Appleby's End* prompts Inspector Matlow, when commenting on the speed of Appleby solving his cases, to say, "I shouldn't be surprised if you get the whole business finally sorted out in the morning. For you must be called a fast worker, Mr. Appleby, if we may judge by the speed with which you've hitched yourself." Indeed, the majority of Appleby's cases are solved in a short period of time.

Judith goes on to accompany Appleby in another fourteen novels and makes appearances in fourteen of the short stories.

Their youngest son Robert (Bobby), an undergraduate and author, eventually assists his father in three novels and one story.

After his marriage, Appleby attempts early retirement, buying the yellow Bentley from Scotland Yard. By the time of *A Private View*, he has a knighthood and is Assistant Commissioner of Scotland Yard. Ten years later, *A Connoisseur's Case* was published and Appleby is now London's Commissioner of Metropolitan Police which is his status when he solves the murder linked with Scroop House. Incidentally, in the previous book, *Silence Observed*, Appleby's age is given as 53 and he is driving an Aston Martin. He and Judith are living in London, five minutes from Whitehall. When we read *Appleby at Allington* (U.S., *Death by Water*, both 1968), Appleby has finally retired but goes on to detect in another dozen books. These later titles still make for very civilised reading, are always entertaining and have a brightness and elegance not found in most modern fiction.

In *Death at the Chase* (1970), the Applebys are now living at Judith's former home, Long Dream Manor, which she has inherited after the death of her cousin, Everard Raven. Many of Appleby's cases take him to some of Britain's grandest homes; Scamnun Court, Urchins, Lark Manor, Scroop House, Tiffin Place, Ashmore Chase, Allington Park, Belrive Priory and Clusters, to name but a few. John Stewart, writing as Michael Innes, in an essay on John Appleby in *The Great Detectives* (and included in this current volume), explains why Appleby so often frequents country estates—having a closed community keeps all the protagonists together under the eye of the detective until it is time for the denouement.

It is a sixty year old Sir John Appleby who is the guest speaker at the Crooks' Colloquium annual dinner in *Appleby's Answer* (1973). The latest crime writer to be elected to Crooks' Colloquium is Miss Priscilla Pringle, author of *Poison at the Parsonage, Revenge at the Rectory*, and others. She features prominently in this engaging story of death at Long Canings in darkest Wiltshire.

In Appleby's final appearance, fifty years on from his debut, he investigates the murder of Lord Osprey in *Appleby and the Ospreys* (U.K.1986, U.S. 1987). At the end of the book, he is standing on the causeway at Clusters watching in horror as bats go about their business. He exclaims, "The creatures hope to make a meal of them ... Good God! Outside—all of us! Ringwood, whistle up your men." John Appleby was decisive to the end.

Besides the detecting talents of the Appleby family, Innes created several series characters but, unfortunately, each made only a few appearances. Detective Inspector Cadover of Scotland Yard, a methodical and routine policeman, detects in *What Happened at Hazelwood, The Journeying Boy* and *A Private View*. He also assists in solving the murder of blackmailer Honoria Clodd in the short story "The Key." In his autobiography, Innes himself comments, "that Cadover is rather a good police detective and easier to believe in, often enough, than is John Appleby."

The fashionable portrait painter and art expert, Charles Honeybath R. A., features in *The Mysterious Commission* (U.K. 1974, U.S. 1975), *Honeybath's Haven, Lord Mullion's Secret* (1981) and *Appleby and Honeybath* (1983). In *Honeybath's Haven*, the artist is keen to discover the reason for the drowning of his friend and fellow artist Edwin Lightfoot. The story is great fun, introducing several seemingly dotty people at Hanwell Court, a home for the elderly, where the body is found.

Hildebert Braunhopf, the art dealer and proprietor of the Da Vinci Gallery, is in *A Private View, Money From Holme* (U.K. 1964, U.S. 1965), *A Family Affair* (U.S., *Picture of Guilt*, 1969). Braunhopf also appears in two short stories, "The Exile" in which paintings are stolen from his gallery, and "The Heritage Portrait" where an artist is shot because of what he has painted.

Dr. Giles Gott is the Junior Proctor and fellow of St. Anthony's College. As well as being an eminent Elizabethan scholar, he writes mystery stories under a pseudonym. He and Colonel Tommy Pride, a chief constable, both make meaningful contributions to the novels.

The thirteen non-Appleby books by Michael Innes contain some fine examples of his work. *What Happened at Hazelwood* is solved by Inspector Cadover as he investigates the murder of Sir George Simney. This is a masterly whodunit with a country house setting.

Cadover also appears in *The Journeying Boy*, which, along with *The Man From the Sea* (1955), is an excellent thriller in the style of John Buchan.

"Colonel Petticate stared at his wife in stupefaction. He could scarcely believe the evidence of his eyes—or of the fingers which he had just lifted from her pulse. But it was true. The poor old girl was dead." Thus begins the stylishly written *The New Sonia Wayward*. Petticate has been living off his wife's earnings as a bestselling writer of romantic fiction. As her death takes place on their yacht, he decides to dispose of the body at sea. He resolves to finish his wife's current novel and continue with others, pocketing all the earnings. Obviously, it does not turn out to be as easy as this. This very clever, ironic and humorous novel involves theft, blackmail, impersonation and attempted murder; a classic Innes.

J. I. M. Stewart wrote several straightforward novels and short stories under his own name. He admitted that it took eight or nine months to write each novel, as opposed to the Michael Innes books, which he wrote in about six weeks. The first novel, *Mark Lambert's Supper*, was published in 1954. This was then followed by ten more novels; Stewart then wrote *The Gaudy*, the first in a popular and well received quintet which had an overall title of *A Staircase in Surrey*. The five books, published between 1974 and 1978, have an Oxford setting and their central figure is Duncan Pattullo, a Scottish playwright. In *Myself and Michael Innes*, Stewart states that "with the possible exception of my volume in the *Oxford History of English Literature*, this quintet represents my most sustained single effort as a writer." Other novels and stories followed.

Stewart also published books on Joseph Conrad, Thomas Hardy, Rudyard Kipling and William Shakespeare. He worked for many years on *Eight Modern Writers*, a volume for *The Oxford History of English Literature*.

Seventy-four short stories were written under the Michael Innes pseudonym. Only one of these stories does not feature John Appleby and it is collected at the end of this volume. Three previous collections of short stories have been published: *Appleby Talking* (U.S.,

Dead Man's Shoes, both 1954), *Appleby Talks Again* (1956) and *The Appleby File* (U.K. 1975, U.S. 1976). See the Appendix for details.

In all, twenty-five stories involve murder. Victims are variously dispatched by poison, shooting, being smothered, stabbed, bludgeoned, pushed from a window or drowned. In one case, the murderer gets away with it. Excellent examples of Innes's skill in constructing a short story are "Pokerwork," "The Furies," "Eye Witness," "A Small Peter Pry," "The Key," "Tragedy of a Handkerchief," "The Exile," "False Colours," "The Heritage Portrait," "Pelly and Cullis," "The Ascham" and "Lesson in Anatomy".

During the 1950's, the London *Evening Standard* newspaper regularly featured detective stories, especially written for the paper, by acknowledged leading writers in the genre. In the year 1950, the contributing authors included Margery Allingham, Leo Bruce, Edmund Crispin, Freeman Wills Crofts, Cyril Hare, E. C. R. Lorac, Philip Macdonald, Gladys Mitchell, Clayton Rawson, John Rhode, Julian Symons, Roy Vickers and Clifford Witting.

Michael Innes supplied many stories to the *Evening Standard* right through the fifties (see the Appendix) and some were illustrated by artists such as Keith Mackenzie and Leonard. Many of the stories were published under various series titles: "Appleby's Fables," "Deckchair Detective," "The Mystery Club" and "Appleby's Holidays."

The collection presented here spans the period 1954–1979 and contains the remaining uncollected stories of Michael Innes. Seventeen of the stories in *Appleby Talks About Crime* are spread across the long, successful career of Appleby from his time as an Inspector to when he is Sir John, the Commissioner of the Metropolitan Police, and then through to his retirement. Judith Appleby is present in two of the stories. Several of the stories concern theft, be it of emeralds, manuscripts, paintings, diamonds or letters. Murders by poison and shooting occur. Six of the stories are centred around The Mystery Club. The six members, which include Sir John Byatt, a surgeon, Elrick, a solicitor, Plumbridge, an artist and Warriner, a Foreign Office official, meet regularly to solve various mysteries.

As a long-time admirer of the Michael Innes books, it has been a privilege for me to gather the stories in this volume. I hope this collection of rediscovered gems by Michael Innes will give you, the reader, as much pleasure as I have had in putting *Appleby Talks About Crime* together.

John Cooper
Westcliff-on-Sea
14 July 2009

JOHN APPLEBY

JOHN APPLEBY

JOHN APPLEBY came into being during a sea voyage from Liverpool to Adelaide. Ocean travel was a leisured affair in those days, and the route by the Cape of Good Hope took six weeks to cover. By that time I had completed a novel called *Death at the President's Lodging* (*Seven Suspects* in the U.S.A.) in which a youngish inspector from Scotland Yard solves the mystery of the murder of Dr. Umpleby, the president of one of the constituent colleges of Oxford University. It is an immensely complicated murder, and Appleby is kept so busy getting it straight that he has very little leisure to exhibit himself to us in any point of character or origins. But these, in so far as they are apparent, derive, I am sure, from other people's detective stories. I was simply writing a yarn to beguile a somewhat tedious experience—and in a popular literary kind at that time allowable as an occasional diversion even to quite serious and even learned persons, including university professors. (It was to become a rather juvenile university professor that I was making this trek to the Antipodes.)

Appleby arrives in Oxford in a "great yellow Bentley"—which suggests one sort of thriller writing, not of the most sophisticated sort. But "Appleby's personality seemed at first thin, part effaced by some long discipline of study, like a surgeon whose individuality has concentrated itself within the channels of a unique operative technique." This is altogether more highbrow, although again not exactly original. And Appleby goes on to show himself quite formidably educated, particularly in the way of classical literature. "The fourteen bulky volumes of the Argentorati Athenaeus" (and for that matter Schweighaüser's edition of the *Deipnosophists*) he takes quite in his stride when he encounters them in Dr. Umpleby's study. This must be regarded as a little out of the way in a London bobby lately off the beat. And there is no sign that Appleby is other than this; he is not the newfangled sort of policeman (if indeed such then existed) recruited from a university. Research in this volume will show that he is definitely not himself an Oxford man. This has frequently been a contentious issue, and I fear that the evidence becomes a shade confused in some later chronicles.

What Appleby does possess in this early phase of his career is (I am inclined to think) a fairly notable power of orderly analysis. Had he been a professor himself, he would have made a capital expository lecturer. But I am far from claiming that he long retains this power; later on he is hazardously given to flashes of intuition, and to picking up clues on the strength of his mysteriously acquired familiarity with recondite artistic and literary matters. He also becomes rather fond of talking, or at least of frequenting the society of persons who prefer amusing conversation to going through the motions of being highly suspicious characters, much involved with low life and criminal practice.

What I am claiming here (the reader will readily perceive) is that Appleby is as much concerned to provide miscellaneous and unassuming "civilized" entertainment as he is to hunt down baddies wherever they may lurk. And I think this must be why he has proved fairly long-lived: and by this I mean primarily long-lived in his creator's imagination. In forty years I have never quite got tired of John Appleby as a pivot round which farce and mild comedy and parody and freakish fantasy revolve.

If I finished the first of these stories before reaching Australia, I think I am right in my reckoning when I say that I had written a dozen of them before coming away again ten years later. This suggests more application than, I fear, actually went into the activity; one is rather freely inventive when one is young, and the stories seemed to get themselves on the page out of odd corners of my mind at odd times and seasons. I never brooded over them as I was to brood over ordinary "straight" novels later; and here I was only being faithful to that first *ethos* of the "classical" English detective story as a diversion to be lightly offered and lightly received. Yet the circumstances of my diurnal life and my immediate physical and social surroundings during those years must have had some impact upon them. Where did this lie?

I think a species of naive nostalgia was at work. English life and manners had a compelling fascination for me—and the more so because, as a Scot who had scarcely crossed the border as a boy, my experience of them had been comparatively brief. And at once keen but impressionistic! So as Appleby moves through his early adventures he reflects something of this situation. He is within a society remembered rather than observed—and remembered in terms of literary conventions which are themselves distancing themselves as his creator works. His is an expatriate's world. It is not a real world, controlled by actual and contemporary social pressures, any more than is, say, the world of P. G. Wodehouse.

But the sphere of Appleby's operations is conditioned by other and, as it were, more simply technical factors. Why does he move, in the main, through great houses and amid top people: what an Englishman might call the territory of *Who's Who?* It might be maintained that it is just because he likes it that way. We never learn quite where he comes from. He has a sister who has been an undergraduate at Oxford, and an aunt of somewhat imperious aristocratic manners who lives in Harrogate; he has married into an eccentric family, the Ravens, who are country gentry. But wherever he comes from (and it appears to me to be some quite simple station of life), he is a highly assimilative person, who moves, or has learned to move, with complete assurance in any society. Eventually he makes a very convincing commissioner of Metropolitan Police, which is Britain's highest job in a police service. I'm not sure that he isn't more verisimilar in this role than he is as a keen young detective crawling about the floor looking for things. So one might aver that he finds his way into all those august dwellings because he fancies life that way.

But this isn't quite the fact of the matter. In serious English fiction, as distinct from a fiction of entertainment, the great house has long been a symbol—or rather a microcosm—of ordered society; of a complex, but on the whole harmonious, community. And indeed French, Russian, and American novelists have tended to see life that way; in the "English" novel the grandest houses of all have been invented by Henry James.

Something of this has rubbed off on the novel's poor relation, the detective story—the more readily, perhaps, because in England itself that sort of story was in its heyday rather an upper-class addiction.

But Appleby, like many of his fellow-sleuths in the genre, roams those great houses for a different and, as I have said, technical reason. The mansion, the country seat, the ducal palace, is really an extension of the sealed room, defining the spatial, the territorial boundaries of a problem. One can, of course, extract a similar effect out of a compact apartment or a semidetached villa. But these are rather cramping places to prowl in. And in detective stories detectives and their quarry alike must prowl. At the same time, they mustn't get lost. And this fairly spacious unity, the Unity of Place in Aristotle's grand recipe for fiction, conduces to an observance of those other unities of time and action which hold a fast-moving story together. And just because Appleby is leisured and talkative, urbane and allusive; just because he moves among all those people with plenty to say themselves; just because of this he wisely seeks out that rather tight *ambiance*.

There is one other point that strikes me about him as I leaf through his chronicles. They *are* chronicles in the sense that time is flowing past in them at least in one regard. The social scene may be embalmed in that baronets abound in their libraries and butlers peer out of every pantry. But Appleby himself ages, and in some respects perhaps even matures. He ages along with his creator, and like his creator ends up as a retired man who still a little meddles with the concerns of his green unknowing youth.

A SMALL PETER PRY

A SMALL PETER PRY

THAT PAINTING?" Appleby glanced at a small landscape—it might have been a glimpse of the Seine at Polssy—which hung above his collection of professional relics. The main point about it, as you might guess, is its being a forgery. It purports to be by the ill-fated Peter Pry."

"Good lord!" I was impressed. "Wasn't that a very queer affair?"

"Decidedly. And I came into it myself in rather a queer way too. Every now and then, you know, I go over to Paris for routine contacts with some of the people at the *Sûreté*. On the occasion I'm thinking of my wife had come with me, and we were planning to go straight down to Antibes for a holiday afterwards. But the *affaire* Pry intervened.

"For the few days that my business appeared likely to detain me, we parked ourselves at St. Germain. To my mind, if not to Judith's, our hotel was on the gorgeous side, but it was at least convenient for that marvellous terrace and view. When I mentioned this choice of ours to any of my Parisian colleagues they would compliment me on the excellent taste which had dictated it and recommend this or that walk in the forest. I think it was on my third day that one of them casually added, as if merely touching on one more of the attractions of the place, that an Englishman had just been mysteriously shot there."

"In the forest?"

"No—in a sort of garden-pavilion, I gathered, of one of the other hotels in the town. I wasn't terribly interested. Or rather I was politely uninterested at once. I had no intention of starting my holiday by assisting in the investigation of a nice little English-style crime in foreign parts. My informant took the hint—they are a perceptive people—and no more was said."

Appleby paused, and let his glance rest on the little painting as if just struck by something of fresh interest in it. "But you did investigate, all the same?" I prompted.

"In a sense I did. That afternoon, when I got back to St. Germain, I found Judith taking tea on the terrace with a totally strange woman—and behaving very irresponsibly, I'm sorry to say."

"Irresponsibly?"

"That expensive hotel was stuffed with wealthy Americans—and Judith was pretending to be one of them. It is something she can do very well. The conversation was about art—about how beautiful art is, and where it can be purchased for export on the most advantageous terms. I sat down and said very little. But as that is no more than the common behaviour of the American husband in such circumstances the illusion wasn't spoilt. And presently I was rather amused. For it was clear to me that what I was listening to was sales-talk."

I was puzzled by this. "You mean that Lady Appleby—"

"No, no." Appleby was delighted by this blunder on my part. "Judith is an artist, it's true. But on this occasion she was cast for the role of customer—wealthy American customer. It was being intimated to her that if she was sufficiently discreet and clever and enterprising, she might have a chance of picking up a Peter Pry at a real bargain price. For Pry was living quietly in St. Germain at that very moment, and in circumstances which might make him glad of a little ready cash."

"This woman talking to your wife claimed to know him?"

"She was claiming in a delicate way to be Pry's mistress, and surrounding his situation with a great deal of mysterious talk. I was interested, I confess. It's a well-known type of fraud nowadays, but I hadn't happened to run up against it myself before."

"Fraud?" I was perplexed. Appleby nodded. "It's no longer much good faking old masters, because customers are getting to know about the various scientific tests that can be applied. But bogus contemporary paintings are less vulnerable, and there is this regular technique for marketing them. The forger starts by concocting a small collection of some famous artist's supposed work.

Then, for a time, he impersonates the artist—and has a woman such as this that Judith had picked up, who goes quietly round bringing in guileless purchasers. Commonly there is some hush-hush story that accounts for the covert nature of the whole thing. The purchaser probably gets an additional kick out of that. It makes him feel that he's had a glimpse of Bohemian life."

"And this woman made it all plausible—about Pry, I mean?"

"Remarkably so. You could have known quite a bit about Pry and still been impressed. She made discreet play with his being a thoroughly unstable personality—particularly given, as you may have heard, to terrific hates and vendettas. It seemed a shame not to be led up the garden path by this ingenious lady, and in the end Judith and I went along. I was uncommonly curious to see the pseudo-Pry and his spurious creation.

"Well, we found him in an uninviting little atelier in the Rue de Pontoise. He didn't seem to have much English, which was odd in an English painter, but the lady explained that he was suffering a quite staggering bout of artistic temperament. He was as startlingly savage, I'm bound to say, as the authentic Pry could well have been. We looked at the paintings, and I bought one. There it is." And Appleby pointed to the wall.

"Bought what you knew to be a fake?" I was surprised.

"Just a collector's instinct, my dear chap. By which I mean the policeman's instinct to collect evidence. It was a transaction which could eventually land our enterprising friends in jail. And I suppose I should eventually have gone ahead to that end had not quite a new fact emerged. My colleague at the *Sûreté* had occasion to ring me up just before dinner. And at the end of our talk he mentioned—once more quite casually—that the Englishman who had been found shot in that garden-pavilion was now known to be Joseph Diplock, one of the largest picture dealers in London."

"So the plot, in fact, thickened." I offered this with reasonable confidence. "What did you do?"

"I ventured to give my French colleague a little advice. Then I got through to London and collected, without much difficulty, some information which you may already guess. The unfortunate

Diplock had controlled virtually all the marketing of Pry's pictures—and by Pry, of course. I mean the real Pry."

I nodded. "And what did you do then?"

"Do then?" Appleby seemed surprised. "Why, nothing at all. The affair was finished, so far as I was concerned, and could have only one conclusion. Don't you see?"

From Appleby, this is not a question that I always care for. But on the present occasion I spoke up boldly enough. "I think I do. Diplock had got wind of the imposture that was being perpetrated at the expense of his client and had gone to St. Germain to expose it. Where upon the false Pry killed him."

Appleby shook his head. "Don't you notice something that rules that out? It was *after* the death of Diplock that Judith and I were lured into the false Pry's little parlour—and just in the common way of business. It was quite incredible that with blood on their hands, and the certainty of Diplock's identity and connections being traced, they should have been placidly continuing their profitable little game."

"But if they were innocent, then I don't see—"

"The advice I gave to the fellow at the *Sûreté* was to have the ports watched for the real Pry slipping quietly back to England. For the only conceivable explanation lay *there*. It was the real Pry who had got wind of the fraud being carried on at St. Germain, and it was at his instigation that Diplock crossed over to investigate.

"Pry quietly followed. He had developed one of his wholly unbalanced hatreds of the dealer, and now he had seen a means of eliminating him—and perhaps of eliminating the fellow who was uttering the forged Prys too. His mistake lay in not making sure that the false Pry should hear at once of the killing of Diplock. Had the false Pry done so, he would almost certainly have taken alarm and fled—and then the case against him would have been so clear that nobody would have started thinking about the movements of the real Pry at all."

"They caught the real Pry?"

"Certainly. He was ill-fated, as I said."

THE AUTHOR CHANGES HIS STYLE

THE AUTHOR CHANGES HIS STYLE

"I SEEM to have heard of such things happening in America," I said. Appleby nodded. "Well, yes. Sometimes an author there meets with sudden and quite staggering financial success. And he just can't take it, and proceeds to blow his brains out. But it wasn't like that with Dobson here in London. It's true that Dobson had achieved marked success—and rather late in his career as a writer. But his new standing had already been an established fact for several years."

"He'd rather altered his manner of writing, hadn't he?"

"Very decidedly. His earlier books had been high-brow and difficult. Then he changed, and produced three short novels of a much more popular sort. But they were genuinely good—quite dazzlingly good—of their kind.

"The most distinguished critics had expressed a high respect for Raymond Dobson's later work. So it might be said that he was sitting very pretty. As a matter of fact the third of those novels, *Meeting at Mâcon,* had just been published—and was clearly in for a big success—when the thing happened. You recall the circumstances?"

I shook my head. "I don't think I ever heard about them."

"Dobson had put in a quiet morning working in his study. A batch of press-cuttings had come in by the first post, and he had given some time to pasting them into an album. It was a job he liked doing himself."

"He was a conceited sort of chap?"

"Possibly you might call him that. But vanity is a widespread trait among authors. They like to linger over laudatory notices, even when they know they mean very little. Anyway, that was what Dobson had been doing. Then he walked into his secretary's room and told her to ring up the police.

"She was puzzled, and asked what she was to tell them. 'Tell them they're needed here,' Dobson said. Then, just as the secretary had got through to the local station, he produced an old army revolver and shot himself dead."

"Wasn't that rather inconsiderate?" I asked.

"It was. The poor young woman appeared to get a terrible shock. When the police did arrive, they found her flat on the floor. Her name, by the way, was Grace Shaw. She hadn't been with Dobson long. But she seemed very much affected, all the same."

I considered this beginning of Appleby's narrative for some seconds. "I distrust your Grace Shaw," I said.

My friend laughed. "Well, you must distrust someone. And, so far, Grace is the only person available. She doesn't require much documenting. She'd worked for a publisher, she'd worked for a printer, and she'd spent a couple of years in some unknown job in Paris. Later, Dobson took her on. He was a bachelor, and she simply went in by the day. It was all perfectly respectable. Indeed, there seemed nothing about Dobson that wasn't."

"No background for blackmail, or anything like that?"

"I couldn't discover any. And his doctor assured me that he was in perfectly sound health."

"Overwork, and a fit of depression—something like that?"

"There was no sign of it. And Dobson wasn't a purely sedentary type. In fact, he'd done some pretty adventurous things. Did you ever hear of a young Australian called Ron Lewis? He was a Sydney man, who had spent a couple of years on the continent and begun to make a bit of a name for himself as a poet. He and Dobson—who was much older—became acquainted, and decided to do some exploring together."

This stirred some recollection in my mind. "Persia?" I asked.

"Yes, Persia. Perhaps exploring is too grand a term for their proceedings. They took a car with some notion of motoring pretty well all the way to Australia. But in Persia young Lewis caught some bug and died. Dobson was said to have behaved very well. He put up a tough fight for his young friend's life. And then, when it was all over, he went on to Australia, saw Lewis's people, and said and did all the right things."

"Did the experience," I asked, "have any effect on Dobson's writing?"

"Well it was after Lewis's death—which had apparently been a pretty ghastly business—that his books took on their new tone. Superficially, it was rather surprising. You might have expected a *deepening* of tone—but the actual transition was to something *lighter.* Acute critics said that Dobson's ordeal had enabled him to quit trying to be something he was not, and to write in a simple and unaffected way."

Again I considered the course of Appleby's story. "Raymond Dobson's writing," I said, "seems to remain in the picture. Did it turn out to have a key place in the mystery?"

Appleby shook his head.

"Raymond Dobson's writing," he said, "turned out to have no place in the mystery at all. But Ron Lewis's did."

"The young man's poetry?" I asked.

"No, not his poetry." But let me tell you how I worked it all out. It wasn't a spectacular process; it was a thoroughly plodding one. I began by tracing Dobson's movements back, month by month and year by year, until I had a fairly good notion of them over a period of some six years all told. And I discovered one curious thing. He appeared never to have been in Burgundy."

I stared. "Burgundy? Dobson was interested in wine?"

"An interest in wine might, of course, taken you to Mâcon— although you'd be more likely to frequent the Côte d'Or itself, rather farther north. But the point of interest was rather different.

"*Meeting at Mâcon* didn't strike me as a book written by a man who hadn't been there. In fact it was the work of somebody with the place pretty fresh in his mind. That was queer, wouldn't you say?"

"Very queer indeed."

"The next step I'll tell you about is simply one among a great many that I took more or less in the dark. I cabled to the police in Sydney. They discovered that Ron Lewis, although he had been away from his people for so long, was a dutiful and regular correspondent. And there were letters from Mâcon stretching over something like a couple of months."

"My dear Appleby—theft! Plagiarism!"

"Quite so. Lewis had written three short novels. But he was a perfectionist, and he hadn't been able to bring himself to take any steps towards publishing them. They were with him on the Persian journey, and Dobson found them after his death. Later, when Dobson went on to Sydney, he made sure that Lewis's people had no inkling of the novels' existence."

"So there was an enormous temptation?"

"Yes. Dobson realised at once the quality of the work that had come so strangely into his hands. And he stole it."

I turned it all over in silence. "And he was stricken by shame and remorse, and so made away with himself?"

"Not precisely that. He had learnt from Lewis that there had been nobody in Europe in his confidence; nobody who knew anything about any of his writings. But that hadn't been quite true. Lewis was concealing something—something he didn't want to talk about.

"In Paris he had been in love with a young English girl called Grace Shaw. And she had in fact had some glimpses of the manuscripts of the books. When she came upon the first of them after its publication, with Dobson's name on the title page, she at once suspected the truth. The appearance of the second book confirmed her suspicion. Of course she was powerless to prove anything. But eventually she managed to get that job with Dobson."

"And *then*?" I asked.

Appleby smiled grimly. "Can't you guess?"

"Certainly I can't guess."

"Those press-cuttings. They weren't all just laudatory reviews of *Meeting at Mâcon*. One was from a Sydney newspaper. Or at least it looked as if it was. Grace, remember, had worked with a printer, and could easily get a bogus clipping prepared—no doubt with some vague story of a joke. And she slipped it into the batch that morning."

"Whatever did it say?"

"It announced the discovery—to the surprise of his family—of a quantity of manuscript material in the handwriting of Ron Lewis, a young poet whose career had been cut short by his death in Persia. What was in question appeared to be the drafts of several novels, including one set in a small wine-growing town in the south of France. The material was being examined by a Professor of Literature at Sydney University."

"So Dobson knew it was all up?"

"He *thought* it was all up. When he had shot himself, the girl of course destroyed the bogus cutting. Her lover was avenged."

I managed to smile. Appleby, I must own, was beginning to get on my nerves. "It's such a horrible story," I said, "that I've no doubt it leads you to some highly edifying conclusion."

But Appleby shook his head. "This one," he said, "is like Dr. Johnson's *Rasselas*. It has a conclusion in which nothing is concluded. Good night."

THE PERFECT MURDER

THE PERFECT MURDER

"MY DEAR brother's death was, of course, a great grief to me," Miss Filby offered this, in a wholly comfortable tone, towards the end of her little party. The interval that had elapsed since Sir Rupert's decease could now undoubtedly be reckoned in months rather than weeks; and the party had decidedly not been uproarious. Nevertheless, it was possible to feel that Miss Filby was setting out to enjoy life, if necessarily in an unspectacular and middle-aged way.

"I gather," Appleby said, "that it was very sudden?" He spoke vaguely, while hunting for his hat. Leaving her remaining guests, Miss Filby had accompanied him into her high, gloomy hall.

"Entirely unexpected. And . . . and such frightful pain."

Miss Filby's voice had changed. Appleby, glancing at her quickly, saw that the general comfortableness of her new life was in fact haunted by some spectre. "I'm very sorry to hear that," he said gravely, "but at least Sir Rupert didn't suffer for long."

"No more than an hour—but it was enough." Miss Filby hesitated. "You don't know about it? Poor Rupert came home one evening—I never discovered from where—and appeared to be perfectly well. Fifteen minutes later, this—this agony came on, and lasted for an hour. But it was quite enough."

"And then he died?"

"Yes. And no cause was ever discovered. That, you see, was the second awful thing. Since Rupert was so famous a chemist, it was thought that conceivably he had ingested—taken—something fatal in his laboratory. But the post mortem revealed nothing at all, no cause of death, no organ or function apparently disordered in the slightest degree." Miss Filby's voice shook. "It was the body of a man who ought not have been dead."

It must have been trying, Appleby thought, for the fellows in the path tab. But again some remark was called for. "I'm very sorry,"

41

it occurred to him to say, "that I never had a chance of knowing so distinguished a man as your brother better."

Miss Filby was pleased. "You would have had much in common." She said. "Rupert took a keen amateur interest in criminology. Might I show you his books? I should very much like to."

Having of necessity responded with a civil murmur, Appleby found himself conducted into a large, dead, and carefully dusted library. Miss Filby moved to a corner. "There!" she said triumphantly.

Appleby glanced first at one shelf and then at several more. "But my dear Miss Filby," he said in astonishment, "these are simply detective stories—hundreds and hundreds of them!"

"Isn't it the same thing?" Miss Filby was not at all put out. "Rupert was a great authority on them. And—do you know?—he even wrote one."

"Dear me, I'm afraid I haven't read it. You must tell me the title, so that I can get hold of it."

Miss Filby shook her head "It was never published."

"Really?" Appleby imported the proper mild regret into his reply to this insignificant intelligence. "But why not?"

"I never knew. I suppose it wasn't clever enough."

"I see." The ingenuous absurdity of this made Appleby want to laugh. But he added gravely: "Has the manuscript been preserved?"

"Oh, no! I saw Rupert burn it myself. But he gave me no explanation, apart from saying that he had consulted a friend."

"Was that do you think, before he had shown it to anyone else—a publisher, for instance?"

"That was my impression. I was disappointed, since it would have been amusing for Rupert to launch out with a new hobby. But I don't think it was ever mentioned between us again."

Appleby was looking at Miss Filby with an absent frown. Presently he asked a final question. "How long ago was this?"

"Oh—comparatively recently. Certainly not more than a couple of years before Rupert's death."

It was a week later than Appleby called on Dr. Taverner.

"I understand," he said when he had introduced himself, "that your uncle, Julius Taverner, died suddenly about a month ago?"

"That is so." Taverner, who was seated behind a large desk in his handsome study, looked at Appleby attentively. "It was quite unexpected, and might almost be called mysterious which is the reason, I suppose, that you are making official inquiries?"

"I'm not doing that." Appleby shook his head emphatically "Indeed, I am doing no more than following up, quite privately, an obscure speculation of my own."

Taverner's eyes narrowed "This is surprising. But proceed."

"I don't know whether you were acquainted, Dr. Taverner with the late Sir Rupert Filby?"

For a fraction of a second Taverner hesitated. Then he bowed. "Certainly," he said smoothly, "Rupert Filby was a very old friend of mine. You know the family?"

"Filby himself I knew only slightly. But Miss Filby I know quite well."

"This is most interesting." Taverner rose and with cordiality steered Appleby to an armchair by the fire. "We shall be more comfortable here," he said. "May I offer you a glass of sherry?"

"Thank you. I shall be delighted."

"Splendid." Taverner went off and busied himself for a moment in a corner of the room, and Appleby took a little stroll towards a window. They met again before the fireplace. Taverner carrying a silver salver with two handsome crystal glasses already filled with brown sherry. "Or would you have preferred Madeira?" he asked. "I can get it in a moment."

Appleby shook his head, and Taverner set down the salver between them. "Yes," he said. "Poor Rupert Filby. It was very sudden, that." He frowned. "By jove—you don't think it connects up in some way with my Uncle Julius? They had uncommonly similar ends."

For a moment Appleby was silent. "Dr. Taverner," he presently asked, "when did Filby show you his detective story?"

Taverner jumped to his feet—and at the same moment there came a thunderous knocking at his front door. He swirled round and strode to the window, and then turned back, shaking.

"Only a telegraph-boy," he muttered. "Funny way to behave." He picked up his sherry with an unsteady hand and drained it. Then he looked at Appleby's empty glass. "It won't do," he said suddenly. "You've got nothing—and now you never will have."

Appleby, too, was looking at his own empty glass—and then he glanced at Taverner's. "I'm so sorry," he said, "but, while you were at the window. I was admiring these glasses. And I'm afraid I accidentally switched them round. Do you mind?"

"You devil!" Taverner's voice was a high scream. Before Appleby could intervene he had snatched a pistol from his pocket, thrust it into his mouth, and pulled the trigger. Within seconds he was dead.

An explanation was owing to Miss Filby. "You see," Appleby said, "your brother, being a great research chemist, happened to discover what is, in a way, the detective-story writer's dream: the absolutely undetectable way of committing murder."

"The poison unknown to science?"

"Much more than that. The *untraceable* poison unknown to science. He wrote his story round it, and showed the result to Taverner. Taverner at once pointed out the fatal flaw. Unless the true formula was given in the story, the effect would be unconvincing and feeble. Actually to give it, on the other hand, would be tantamount to putting an invincible weapon in the hands of every criminal in the country.

"It can't, of course, really have needed Taverner to tell your brother this: and that's why the story had to be destroyed. But Taverner had noted the formula and when he wanted his uncle Julius out of the way, he planned to use it. But to do so with your brother alive would be too risky."

"My brother would certainly have known that Dr. Taverner, as Julius Taverner's heir, would inherit a large fortune from him."

"Precisely. And your brother might have drawn conclusions—and so your brother had to go first. When I appeared to draw conclusions. I had to go also."

"You!" Miss Filby was horrified.

"He tried to get me with a glass of sherry as soon as I had hinted that I was inquiring quite on my own. I emptied it on the carpet while his attention was distracted—"

"You had arranged the distraction?"

"I had indeed, since his likely plan of campaign was pretty clear to me. Then by way of frightening him into confession, I pretended I'd switched glasses. I'd forgotten about his almost certain terror at the coming pain." Appleby rose. "But I suppose a quick end was best for him. And the formula, let us be thankful, has perished, too."

THE SCATTERGOOD EMERALDS

THE SCATTERGOOD EMERALDS

I T'S TRUE," Appleby said, "that from one case and another I have kept a good many odds and ends.

"Most of them are quite colourless, and make no great show on the shelf. It's only the stories behind them that have a lurid tint here and there."

"Nothing." I asked as I glanced at the little criminological museum, "at all spectacular in itself?"

"Only this." Appleby took down a plain silver casket, opened it, and tumbled its contents on a table. I blinked, for it was like looking at a little cascade of green fire. Indeed, I actually felt for a moment that he was going to burn himself when he put in a finger and stirred the little pile.

"Did you ever hear of the Scattergood emeralds?"

"The old Marchioness took very little interest in jewellery." Appleby had settled down to tell his story. "She was a strong-minded woman given to practical philanthropy, both on the family estates and in the world at large. But there were formal occasions, of course, upon which she had to appear *en grande tenue,* and then the famous emeralds would be brought out."

"They were an heirloom?" I was staring at the great green stones and wondering how they came to be in Appleby's charge.

"Oh, decidedly. They had been a gift from Charles II when he was something of a family friend. Their extreme value worried Lady Scattergood, and she was for selling them and applying the proceeds to improving various agricultural properties. But the Marquess—whether veraciously or not—declared that he wasn't legally entitled to part with them. And at that Lady Scattergood decided on a course that would make the things at least less of a nuisance to her than they had been. She commissioned the manufacture of replicas."

At this light dawned on me. I pointed to the jewels on the table—and, as I did so, persuaded myself that they were rather less lustrous than I had at first imagined. "In fact, my dear Appleby, these are worthless?"

Appleby smiled, "If you have sufficiently grand ideas you may call them that. Actually, they are worth several hundred pounds. Very high class reproductions of this sort are not inexpensive. But Lady Scattergood felt that her action was going to bring her peace of mind that would be cheap at the price. She had read a lot about burglars, and bandits, and masked men presenting themselves with revolvers at the bedside of titled women. And, although perfectly courageous, she wanted no nonsense of that sort. So she ordered her set of replicas.

"Lord Scattergood quite approved. There might be one or two particularly august occasions in the course of the year, he said, at which it would be proper that the real things should still be worn. But, apart from that, they could remain securely in the bank, and Lady Scattergood go to the opera and what not in the imitations.

"The plan worked very well. Nobody was told—Lord Scattergood didn't care for the idea of its being generally known that his wife went about in paste—and the world might never have been any the wiser but for the burglary."

I was astonished. "Lady Scattergood's apprehensions were really fulfilled?"

"Yes, indeed. A cat burglar carried off the Marchioness's jewellery. She was delighted. I went along to see her myself, and she told me of her stratagem with great *éclat*. So I took my leave and went, straight to the bank."

"The bank, my dear Appleby?" I was nonplussed.

"And I took with me our expert in that sort of thing. It was, you know, an obvious piece of routine. I showed Lady Scattergood's authorization, and the real emeralds were produced. Or rather, that was the idea. Our expert spent 30 seconds on them and declared positively that they weren't the real thing at all. What the bank had been holding were simply high-quality replicas."

"Surely, Appleby, your discovery was a delicate one?"

"It was, indeed. Nothing, I assure you, makes a policeman more cautious than talk of missing heirlooms in a great family. Shocking scandals may always be just round the corner. Still, I hoped for the best—and you can guess what that was."

"Some act of simple carelessness?"

"Just that. Remember that Lady Scattergood, although so proud of her security scheme, didn't really care about the jewels. The formal and ceremonial—not to say the ostentatious—aspect of her social position didn't mean much to her. It seemed quite feasible that she had simply muddled up the true emeralds and the replicas upon some occasion when she had had both beside her. Which was, of course, uncommonly lucky for that cat burglar.

"But somehow I hadn't much confidence in this. Lady Scattergood didn't strike me as a muddle-headed woman. I felt she could have run anything from a jumble sale to a battleship with the same sharp, aristocratic efficiency. And I guessed that her security arrangements would be pretty sound throughout.

"The fellow at the bank made no bones about telling me as much as he knew of the affair at his end. Three times since the emeralds were deposited, Lady Scattergood had called in person to collect them. And on each occasion they had been found, securely locked in their own case, in the bank's night safe on the following morning.

"Lady Scattergood's own account agreed with this entirely. On each occasion the jewels had been taken out to wear at Court. And on each occasion she had collected them herself, and taken them out of their case only when actually ready to put them on. Later she had taken the case down to her car with her, replaced the emeralds in it while driving home—which was done by way of a detour to the bank. And then Lord Scattergood himself had each time nipped out and deposited them in the safe. Well, that was that. I began to have my doubts about the miraculously lucky burglar."

"Doubts, Appleby?" I was much startled. "You mean you doubted his existence?"

"Not at all. He had certainly existed. I simply doubted whether emeralds, true or false, had been any part of his little haul. And

I asked Lady Scattergood a crucial question. When had she last seen the replicas—or what she took to be replicas? Had she looked at them since her last outing in the real thing? And her answer was that she had not. She hadn't had them out of *their* case since a week or so before that—nor subsequently, either.

"At this point I didn't fail to remember an embarrassing fact. Old Lord Scattergood was famous for his eccentric conduct, and there had been some really queer incidents in his past career. Had he quietly pocketed the emeralds that night, returning the replicas to the bank in order to gain a little time before there were any awkward questions? I spent a sleepless night considering this." Appleby smiled. "Which was foolish. Because we caught the burglar next day—with his spoils still in his possession."

"Including the real emeralds?"

"Not at all. Including another set of replicas.

"*This* set." And Appleby began returning the green stones to their case. "Lady Scattergood's cleverness had been her undoing—and right at the start of her operation. The theft had taken place on the premises of the firm making the reproductions, and what had been returned to her were *two* sets of replicas. She wasn't, as I've said, really interested in jewellery, and she never tumbled to the fraud. When, but for that burglar, it would eventually have been detected, one really can't say.

"Did we get back the real emeralds in the end? Oh, dear me, yes. That's why the noble lady gave me these." And Appleby tapped the silver box lightly before returning it to its shelf.

THE IMPRESSIONIST

THE IMPRESSIONIST

THE OTHER day I asked Appleby about the Millicarp affair. He was quite forthcoming. "Millicarp," Appleby said, "was well known as a sculptor. Looking at his work, you would have imagined him to be an uncommonly husky type, sending the splinters flying all over the studio. His carvings in stone had a rough-hewn quality. The whole idea of it, I suppose, was to suggest titanic strength.

"Actually, Millicarp was a puny little fellow—the next thing to a dwarf, and a bit of a cripple as well. This made certain other facts about him all the more surprising. And it made rather more disagreeable, somehow, the business of inspecting his body. Particularly considering the bust. And particularly on a holiday.

"He lived in Cornwall, in the top flat of a young skyscraper of a building in one of those small fishing-towns built round a steep cove. What lay below was rock, and his death was certainly instantaneous."

I stared at Appleby. "He fell out of a window?"

"Either that, or he was pitched out. That was something we had to decide. The bust of Venus didn't really help. It might have been pitched out after him. Or he might have taken it with him, clasped in his arms, with some notion of adding to the momentum of his fall."

"How very unpleasant!"

Appleby smiled grimly. "Well—yes. But it's my trade. Incidentally, there were plenty of other busts and so forth about the place, and we had to ask ourselves if there had been any significance in picking Venus. There was one plausible answer—and again I think you'll call it unpleasant. Millicarp, despite his disabilities, was a pertinacious and successful amorist who had caused no end of trouble in the Bohemian society in which he moved. It looked as if the Venus might have been chucked out after him as a sort of macabre comment on that."

Appleby was silent for a moment, and I shook my head.

"It's not," I said, "an edifying story."

"No, it's not." Appleby looked at me severely. "But didn't you ask for it?"

I was (Appleby said) simply on holiday down there. But the local people called me in at once. I was making my inspection of this displeasing creature's remains within a couple of hours of the thing having happened. The evidence for that is unimportant; it was a matter of fishing-boats going past, and so on. At eight o'clock in the morning the rocks had been clear. By ten, I was examining the body of either a suicide or a murdered man.

It told me very little. If Millicarp had been bruised in any feeble sort of struggle he could have put up against an attacker the effects were not to be distinguished from those of his fall. And his studio didn't tell me much more. It was an untidy place, so that signs of a brief scrap would have been hard to spot. One large window was wide open.

Of the people in the house the one who fixed my attention was a sort of caretaker, called Hill. He seemed a very promising mixture of panic and venom. He just couldn't disguise the fact that he had hated the dead man. And his panic came, so to speak, in patches, whenever the local inspector got on the topic of Millicarp's unflagging interest in women.

Naturally this made me inquire whether there was a Mrs. Hill. That's the way, you know, that a policeman's mind has to work. And, sure enough, a Mrs. Hill was produced. She was an uncommonly good-looking young woman.

I soon didn't have much doubt that she had something to hide— and that her husband had, too. It was just a question of whether it was much or little. Anyway, my local colleague's questions drove her pretty desperate. And it seemed to be as a result of this desperation that she presently produced a suspect for us.

56

She was sure, she said, that Mr. Dale had been down; she was sure she had caught a glimpse of him that morning. And at this her husband promptly said he believed he'd seen Dale, too.

Dale was a painter, it seemed, who lived in London, and who used to come down quite often to visit Millicarp. For instance, he'd been down a week or so before that again, when there had been a spell of blazing hot weather; Mrs. Hill had run into him in a chemist's shop, buying aspirin and olive oil—presumably for sunbathing.

Mrs. Hill had been rather surprised to see him at all on that occasion, for he and Millicarp had lately had an awful row. Mrs. Hill was by way of being too respectable to mention the supposed cause of this. But clearly it was a woman. It might even have been herself.

Well, that was about all we got. And presently I left the local fellows to it and drove straight back to London. But I'd rung through to the Yard before setting out, and arranged for some inquiries to be made. And the painter Dale proved only moderately hard to run to earth.

A squad of men worked on the problem all afternoon as I drove east. And the upshot was that I found myself in Dale's studio—a thoroughly unwelcome visitor—early that summer evening.

Dale was a pale, unhealthy-looking creature, though he was big enough to have thrown Millicarp out of the window. He was painting furiously, in the last of the full light, at a large, complex composition, full of small geometrical forms that seemed to be coming entirely out of his head.

I told him straight away about Millicarp, and he said, "Ah!" in an excited sort of way. But this seemed to be only because he had satisfied himself where some tiny fresh flake of paint should go. Then he did for a moment turn to me.

"It would be that caretaking chap Hill," he said. "Dangerous type. He'd have been upset by Millicarp's making passes at his wife. Disgusting. Glad I washed my hands of that crowd."

And at this Dale went on painting like mad.

I wasn't at all sure he hadn't got hold of the right end of the stick. But of course I wasn't leaving it at that. "They say they saw you," I said.

"Saw me?" Dale turned round on me again, really startled. "Saw me where? And when?"

"Down in Cornwall, Mr. Dale. And early this morning."

"What utter rot!" He gestured at his big, wet canvas. "Even a fool of a policeman can see I've been slaving at this thing all day." And at that Dale grew quite violent. "Get out!" he yelled at me. "Get out, before I throw you downstairs."

Of course this display of temperament interested me and I said something to Dale that really sent him of the deep end. He made a sudden grab at me, slipped, fell backwards, and in doing so brought easel and canvas down with him on the floor.

When he disentangled himself, it was to point at his painting in speechless wrath. This was understandable. His arm must have swept right across the canvas, and a large part of the intricate composition was now no more than a nasty smear.

I examined it. There was not a square inch of it on which the oil paint had even begun to dry out.

"Unfortunate," I said. "Still, you'll agree, Mr. Dale, that it does settle the matter."

THE CLUE to the solution of this mystery has been given.
Who is the murderer?

SOLUTION

"No," Appleby said, "not the caretaker Hill. It was Dale who pitched Millicarp through the window—driven by some crazy jealousy. Of course it certainly did look as if Dale must have been in his London studio all day to have achieved that pretty complicated painting over a large canvas. But you see, he'd really done it the previous week. The pigments hadn't been mixed with any of what painters call the drying oils, which contain metallic salts and begin to harden quickly. They'd been mixed with a non drying medium—one that painters never use because it would never harden. In fact, he'd used that olive oil. It hadn't been for sunbathing—you could tell that from his pasty complexion. And that's why Dale was so clumsy. He just had to stumble and smear the canvas—to convince me of how fresh it was. Unfortunately for him, policemen aren't like some painters, impressionists. They check up. And I did."

THE SECRET IN THE WOODPILE

THE SECRET IN THE WOODPILE

CHARLES LENTON was the dead man's name. He had been a psychiatrist. Inspector John Appleby, viewing what was left of him, unemotionally remarked to Sergeant Aggett that one must expect such chaps to get themselves murdered from time to time.

"Well, yes," Aggett said dubiously. "I suppose you might say, sir, that it's a dangerous job. Constant contact with thoroughly unbalanced types."

"And constant listening to shocking secrets. One might want to rub out somebody in whom one had rashly confided."

"I suppose so." Aggett seemed not particularly impressed. "But that would go for priests as well—the papist ones who hear confessions, that is. And not many priests are murdered."

"Priests don't keep notes. Psychiatrists do. Then one day they give you a fancy name, drape your affairs in a few other perfunctory fictions, and publish your embarrassing past as a case history."

"Not many notes surviving here, sir."

"That's true." Appleby glanced from Lenton's corpse to the wider scene. "And that's our starting point."

One could still see that the spacious consulting room had been handsomely furnished. It was in London's most exclusive medical district. Lenton's practice must have been in a highly lucrative bracket. But the murderer had set the whole place afire in a thoroughly efficient way.

Apart from the body—on which not a stitch remained unconsumed—only ashes, charred wood, and here and there a fragment of curtain or carpet were on view. It was surprising that the building had been saved. But from this floor downward it was as drenched in water as if it had been under the sea.

"It was all antiques, the secretary says," Aggett announced with distaste. "French stuff with fancy names—*armoires*, and the like. A queer way to keep medical records."

"Not much security, certainly. One would expect steel filing cabinets. But I suppose they'd have struck too utilitarian a note."

"That's it, sir. Not that what you might call confidentiality wasn't well guarded in a way. No names, no pack drill. The case histories were all coded, it seems, as far as proper names went, and Lenton carried round a notebook with the key to it always on his own person. But there isn't anything of that left, as you can see. What I'm wondering is why, if there were no names in the files, the killer thought it necessary to burn down the whole works."

"Suppose, Aggett, the criminal is somebody well-known. And suppose some state of affairs he had once confided to Lenton had striking or even bizarre features which might point to him—names or no names. That would answer your point."

"Yes, sir. But there's another thing. A setup like this is deserted at night. The whole building consists of surgeries or consulting rooms or the like, and everybody packs up and goes home. It wouldn't have been too difficult simply to break in and remove or destroy the files. Instead of which the fellow marches in in broad daylight and does this. He was frightened not only of what was in the closets but of what was in Dr. Lenton's head as well."

"There isn't much left in it now. Until the fire got them, the brains must have been mostly on the carpet." Inspector Appleby glanced at the dead man again with composure. So did Sergeant Aggett. They were accustomed to what a heavy revolver can accomplish at close range. "But it's only one possibility, you know, that the chap wanted to destroy incriminating material. He may simply have wanted to possess himself of it—say, for purposes of blackmail. Quite speculatively, it may have been. Then Lenton turned up and surprised him, and the rest followed. By the way, have you gathered anything yet about the nature of Lenton's practice? It might be relevant."

"Only what his secretary says and that was not much more than a string of long words. So I told her to write them down in my notebook. And here it is." Aggett, a most competent officer, produced this record from his pocket and read with care. "'Dr. Lenton's methods were empirical and eclectic. Deep analysis, simple but sustained psychotherapy, prolonged narcosis, medical hypnotism, ECT, insulin shock, psychotropic drugs, abreactive techniques—'"

"All right, Aggett. We'll just say he wouldn't readily acknowledge himself as baffled."

Appleby didn't find out much more about Charles Lenton that day, or indeed for many days to come. There was nothing shady about the doctor. High medical authority vouched for that. Not only was he among that minority of murdered persons who prove to be without dubious associations of one sort or another, he was a man distinguished, among other things, for his insistence on the highest standards of professional conduct. That might of course, as Aggett pointed out, be "all my eye." But somehow Appleby didn't think so.

Any other lead being lacking, it was necessary to inquire about the dead man's current patients. This was a delicate business. The troubles that lead people to seek psychiatric treatment are very often such as few would care to divulge even to the most sympathetic policeman. Not that Appleby was after that exactly. He could do little more than ask these people about Lenton and their impressions of him, rather than about themselves—this while forming his own opinion of them.

And he could be by no means quite certain he had all these sufferers on parade. Lenton's secretary, Miss Nicholson, seemed a capable young woman, and was confident she had produced a complete list out of her head. Her memory, however, went back no more than a couple of years, and this was true of another form of record which turned up in Lenton's home.

The doctor had kept a duplicate engagement book there, scrapping it more or less year by year. But the last two of these diaries were available, and Appleby studied them closely. They confirmed that the secretary's recollection was reliable—except that here and there a name cropped up that meant nothing to her. These names—there were no more than four or five of them—were distinguished by a small pencil mark.

Appleby conjectured that they were the names of patients whom Lenton had seen, for one reason or another, only privately and at home. And Lenton's housekeeper—he had been an unmarried man—confirmed that this appeared to have happened from time to time.

There was nothing heartening in all this. What can one do with a few surnames scribbled in a diary? Very little—except look them up in the London telephone directory, and find each reproduced by the score or the hundred. But Appleby, having drawn a complete blank with Lenton's known patients, was reduced to just that.

Only one name wasn't hopelessly common. It was Woodpile, and that wasn't common at all. There was only one Woodpile, and he turned out to be a university professor. Appleby resolved to have a go at him.

He found Professor Woodpile at work—an untidy man in an untidy room with a view of the British Museum through the window. And Appleby wasted no time.

"Professor Woodpile, you may have read that a certain Dr. Charles Lenton was recently discovered shot dead in his consulting room. I have called to ask if you were acquainted with him."

"Lenton? Charles Lenton?" It was evident that Woodpile was a highly nervous man. "Never set eyes on him."

"I must tell you, Professor, that your name has been found in his current engagement book—apparently as one with whom he had an appointment at his home. You would appear to be the only person in London named Woodpile. I wonder if I may invite you to comment on the circumstance?"

"My cousin. My Canadian cousin." Woodpile gulped violently. "Turned up out of the blue. Never knew I had one. But here he was—in London, and down with some nervous trouble. He wanted me to recommend somebody who might help him. I knew Lenton's name. Had heard he was a very distinguished and well-reputed psychiatrist. So I told my cousin—"

"What's his other name?"

"His other name?" The learned Woodpile appeared completely at sea.

"This cousin's Christian name."

"Oh, that! Arthur. I think it was Arthur."

"Thank you. Please go on."

"But that's all! I gave my cousin Lenton's name, and he went away. Never saw him again. Nor heard from him either."

"Have you any means of tracing this Arthur Woodpile, this wandering Canadian in search of medical aid?"

"Oh, none whatever. Out of the blue, as I said. And back into it again."

"Professor Woodpile, am I right in thinking that your subject is English Literature?"

"Perfectly right. Everybody knows that. Or everybody in my field."

"Quite so. And it is a field concerned with the deliverances of the imagination?"

"I don't understand you. I don't understand you at all."

"I rather think. You do, sir. And I need hardly emphasize that this is a very serious matter. In the light of that would you care to reconsider your statement?"

"Certainly not."

"There is nothing further you wish to say?"

"Yes, there is. Go away and leave me alone."

This had been a most encouraging interview. Hitherto—at least to Appleby's practiced ear—everybody had told the truth. Even those patients of Lenton's who had been obliged to touch or skirt matters of some embarrassment to themselves, even they had faced up to the gravity of the issue. Woodpile, on the other hand, for reasons still known only to himself, had improvised an absurd fiction. Why had he gone to see the dead man? And why did he want to conceal that he had done so?

There might be some perfectly innocent reason for each of these actions. Woodpile had perhaps consulted Lenton in a normal way—yet abnormally in the sense that he had been in a very unstable state. As a consequence of this he had perhaps quarreled violently with his prospective physician, and even made a nuisance of himself on subsequent occasions. And he might now simply be in a panic because of Lenton's violent end.

The perturbed Woodpile was worth following up. Appleby called on an acquaintance named Howard Collins, also a Professor of Literature.

"What's Woodpile's chief line?" he asked.

"He has only one. He's one of those single-subject scholars who get their teeth into a chap and keep them there for life."

"I see. Who's his chap?"

"The poet Richard Furey."

"Surely he's still alive?"

"He is indeed—and immensely old and eminent. Woodpile's two main books are called *Furey: the Poet* and *Furey: the Man*. Perhaps he'll end up with *Furey: the Corpse*. Furey's said to be pretty far gone."

"Physically, do you mean, or mentally?"

"Chiefly the latter, I believe. He's said to be enormously irascible and egotistical. A Grand Old Man of Letters, and so forth."

"Have you any notion how he gets on with Woodpile—this pertinacious critic and biographer? I imagine a great writer might be irritated or even infuriated by a learned hanger-on of that sort."

"I rather think it's not like that." Professor Collins had shaken his head decisively. "Woodpile has really done quite a lot for Furey's reputation. He discovered the early poems, you know. You must remember about that, Appleby."

"I'm afraid I don't. But how can one be said to discover the early work of a poet still living? I'd imagine the poet would do that for himself, if he had a mind to."

"You have a point there. And it's more accurate to say that Woodpile discovered in manuscript both some very early poems that had never been published and some well-known poems in early versions. Surprisingly early, indeed, in Furey's career."

"Furey was precocious?"

"That's precisely what Woodpile revealed—that Furey was far more of a prodigy than, say, Chatterton or Rimbaud. If he had been a musician it wouldn't have been that remarkable. The infant Mozart, and all that. But poets don't get powerfully going in their nurseries. Alexander Pope liked to claim that he lisped in numbers. But Pope fudged the evidence. Isn't this a bit far from your murdered psychiatrist, my dear Appleby?"

"It does sound that way. Do you think Furey would ever have had occasion to consult a mad doctor? That's what the early mental specialists were called. It's a finely ambiguous expression."

"No doubt. But how should I know? All poets are dotty, of course. Possessed by the Muse, or by the divine *furor*, or what have you. But Woodpile's biography records no visits in the neighborhood of Harley Street. But then it wouldn't, would it? It's what they call an official or authorized biography."

Collins paused, then went on, "Would you care to borrow Woodpile's edition of that early stuff? I've got it here in my room somewhere. Very handsomely got up. Facsimiles of manuscripts, portraits of the young genius from the family photograph album, and so forth and so on."

"It scarcely sounds like one of the documents in the case. But I want to tackle the aged Richard Furey, and a spot of homework might be in order. I'd gain merit—don't you think?—if I showed knowledge of the chap's inspired infancy. So I'll accept your very obliging offer."

"Well, John," Judith Appleby asked her husband at their dinner table several days later, "did you gain admittance to the great man?"

"Yes, I did. And it's all over."

"All over?"

"Decidedly so." Appleby, who would have had to be described as looking mildly shaken, poured claret. "I have to ask myself if I mishandled the thing. The Director of Public Prosecutions may ask me that. Or even the Home Secretary himself."

"Nonsense, John!"

"Well, at least the mystery of Dr. Charles Lenton's death is a mystery no longer. But, you see, I presented myself to the aged poet in the character of an admirer. I'd got a tip that he quite liked that. I'd done my prep, as you know, but my pose was a shade rash, all the same. It made it very difficult to get on to the theme of Lenton, as you can imagine.

"Furey proved to be a powerful man still—physically powerful, I mean—but as crazy as they come. A senile craziness. He went off like a gun about himself and held forth for half an hour by my watch. All about his dazzling precocity. I was prepared for that a little by what Howard Collins had told me. But not for its being an obsessional theme.

"The awful thing is that Furey's poetry *is* poetry, and much of it major poetry at that. His reputation is as secure as a reputation in literature can ever be. But all that he had in his head was this lisping-in-numbers stuff—as discovered and celebrated by the tedious Woodpile."

Appleby paused, poured more claret, then paraphrased an old saying. "But there was a secret in the Woodpile. It's been as simple as that."

"John, I know you're tired. But do talk sense."

"Very well. Have you ever seen a stage hypnotist at work?"

"Yes, I have. But what—"

"Describe some of the things you saw him do."

"He'd hypnotize a man from the audience, lay him out flat on three chairs, and then remove the middle one. The man would stay completely rigid, like a girder or tree trunk, supported only by his head and his heels."

"Yes, I've seen that too. Anything else?"

"He'd stick pins in people, and they wouldn't—"

"Yes, yes. More, please."

"He'd tell somebody he was a duck or a hippopotamus, and then—"

"That as well. Anything with a blackboard?"

"A blackboard? I don't think—but yes—"

"That was it, Judith. That was the whole thing. But, before I come to it, I'll tell you about the end of Furey."

"The *end* of Furey?"

"Just that. He's dead. You see, I got on to Lenton, that skilled medical hypnotist, and I went at Lenton hard. Eventually Furey saw that I *knew*. He sprang up, and I thought he was going to murder me. In fact, he *was* going to murder me. Only he had some frightful seizure instead and dropped dead on the instant. I suppose it gives me my niche in English literary history. But it's uncommonly awkward."

And Appleby smiled rather wanly. "To the best of my recollection, Judith, it's something that never happened to me before."

"Years ago"—Appleby had left the table and was composing himself with a cigar—"years ago Furey presented himself to Lenton, professing himself very interested in certain of the phenomena of hypnotism, and proposing a series of experiments—experiments in the composition of poetry. Now, Judith, go back to that blackboard. Your stage hypnotist gets his subject to sign his name. He then tells him he is fifteen years old and gives the same instruction. Up goes the signature in a fifteen-year-old hand. Eventually he gets back to a point at which his subject is struggling with his ABC's.

"Furey suggested his operating, as it were, at about the age of twelve. He provided Lenton simply with a number of titles. Lenton would give the command, 'Compose a poem called So-and-so,' and off Furey would go. But since what he had in his head were mature poems—some published and some unpublished—with these same titles, precisely that was what he wrote out in the hypnotic state. Lenton may well have had a notion of what was going on, but saw it merely in terms of psychological curiosity. He hadn't a clue that any fraud was in the course of preparation."

"John, you don't mean—"

"Of course I do. Furey got away with a substantial little collection of his own adult work in a hand absolutely verifiable as that of his twelfth or thirteenth year. There would be plenty of his schoolboy letters and so forth to validate the handwriting. And then, to cut a long story short, he contrived to plant this material where the industriously researching Woodpile would be sure to happen on it. And thus did the celebrated Richard Furey juvenilia come into being. Its publication had the incidental result of making Woodpile's reputation."

"And then?"

"The late Dr. Lenton was no sort of literary character, and it was years before the penny, you may say, dropped in his head. But he did at length hear of Furey's fame as a uniquely precocious poetic genius. He got hold of a copy of the book I borrowed from Collins, embellished in facsimile with the actual writings which had been produced under his hypnotic nose—but with never a word in the book about the circumstances of their production. He wasn't a fool; he thought the thing out; and he realized that he had been an innocent party in a monstrous deception. The celebrated Alexander Pope had never fudged evidence in just that way."

"And he determined to expose the racket?"

"Just that. He'd been badly used, duped, but he was a man of complete integrity, and he wasn't standing for it. He informed Furey that he intended to expose the entire deception. By this time Furey's whole ego was bound up with his spurious reputation as a prodigy. In a panic, I imagine, he sent for Woodpile and owned up.

"Woodpile panicked too, feeling that when the truth became known his own reputation as a competent and respectable scholar would be in ruins. He went to see Lenton at his home, pleaded with him to keep silent, may have tried to bribe him as well. It was no go. The outraged Lenton was adamant.

"Woodpile reported back to Furey, and Furey acted. He had to destroy Lenton's files. His name wouldn't be in them, but the facts would be plain to read, and could point only to himself. And he had to destroy Lenton too. He was a powerful old maniac, as I said. And he achieved the slaughter."

"John, how do you know all this?"

"I've had it out of the wretched Woodpile. He was in a terrible funk."

"Is he in danger from the law?"

"Probably not. He was no party to the original deception—even if it was a crime, and conceivably it was not. He was simply fooled as Lenton was. Of course, if he did try to buy Lenton's silence, that might be another matter. But it's something which, in the nature of the case, we shall never know."

"But it must all come out at the inquest on Lenton's death?"

"Most certainly. It will be a great literary sensation."

"And Woodpile will be sunk, so far as his reputation goes?"

"Quite possibly not. They're a strange crowd, scholars of that sort. Perhaps he'll write a book called *An Inquiry into Certain Twentieth Century Poetic Forgeries*—something of that kind—and triumphantly rehabilitate himself."

THE GENERAL'S WIFE IS BLACKMAILED

THE GENERAL'S WIFE IS BLACKMAILED

IT WAS Elrick's dinner, and custom required that he should set the ball rolling. So we weren't surprised when he tapped the table.

"It you don't mind," he said, "I'll spin my yarn early—while you're all being good enough to continue your interest in this champagne, as a matter of fact it began—this odd incident I have in mind—with champagne.

"It began that is to say, with a lady I shall call Mrs. Dominey taking courage from the stuff at a dinner party, and murmuring to me over the rim of her glass that she was in deep, deep trouble. I must have reacted suitability, because she came to see me in my office next day."

Elrick paused, and somebody asked a question. "She was more or less a stranger to you?"

"I was her husband's solicitor which looked as if it might conceivably make the situation rather delicate. But of course a family lawyer has to walk some very pretty tight-ropes. And this one certainly led me into a queer puzzle. It's not spectacular, but I hope it will satisfy you as my contribution this evening."

But here I see I must explain about the Mystery Club. It's an entirely modest affair. There are only six members. We dine together from time to time, taking it in turn to play host, and the idea is that each of us should recount something more or less mysterious that has come under his observation since the last meeting.

Nobody is allowed to delve deeper into the past than that, and this has the effect—or is supposed to have the effect—or making everyone keep a sharp eye open for likely material as he goes about his daily affairs.

Most of our stories, I find, come directly from the professional experience of our members. But there is no rule about this. If the teller in fact knows the solution of his mystery he naturally holds it up until his fellow-members have offered whatever guesses come into their minds. If he doesn't know, then, of course, the mystery has sometimes to remain unsolved.

And you will realise that the whole entertainment—for that is what it is—has to move fairly quickly. If half a dozen problems are to be tackled in an evening, none of them can be worried to death!

So we knew now that even Elrick's rather deliberate legal manner wasn't going to hold us up for long.

"Mrs. Dominey is a pretty picture," he went on, "and much younger than her husband, the General. I suspected some indiscretion which was now—so to speak—coming home to roost, and it appeared I wasn't far wrong. Mrs. Dominey confessed that she had been silly about a perfectly fascinating actor called Callaway. Some of you may have heard of him."

Elrick looked round the table, and I nodded. "Rather a good character-actor," I said, "in melodrama. A Chinese dope pedlar one week and a dissipated duke the next."

"That's the chap. Mrs. Dominey, I may say, struck me as not at all clever, and I don't suppose her theatrical taste would be precisely that of the highbrow. She had admired this chap Callaway, whatever the rubbish he was playing in, and had taken to writing him foolish letters. Eventually, to her great joy, she began to get replies; there was a meeting; and the affair eventually ran to quiet little suppers after Callaway's show. The silly goose had covered them up by telling General Dominey some story about regular visits to a sick aunt. I don't know whether any of you can guess the next move in the game."

"Blackmail?" I asked.

"Just that. Before she knew where she was, Mrs. Dominey found her glamorous new friend demanding money. Quite a lot of it. Mrs. Dominey felt it to be very unfair. She hadn't been seduced; she had merely been compromised; and now she had to pay up. Her husband was devoted to her—but she just couldn't risk telling him her humiliating story."

Elrick finished his champagne. "As you may imagine, I didn't find all this particularly staggering. Such things do come a lawyer's way. And the fringes of blackmail aren't commonly hard to deal with. I set about resolving Mrs. Dominey's predicament in a perfectly routine fashion. I was rather in the position of a surgeon recommending a necessary operation. There was this much risk. I explained, and no more—and it was certainly a risk worth taking. I got Mrs. Dominey to write out and sign her story and I locked it up in my private safe in her presence explaining that with any luck it would never be seen again. Having protected myself in this way. I went to call on Callaway. My business of course was to tell him baldly that if Mrs. Dominey ever heard another syllable from him he would infallibly go to gaol. You won't credit my procedure with much subtlety. I can only say that I'd used it a number of times before and never known it fail."

Elrick pushed his glass away and made a whimsical gesture.

"But it failed this time. Callaway grabbed a telephone and proposed to call up *his* solicitor. I had marched in on him, he said, with an outrageous slander, and he proposed to seek legal redress. He seemed extremely angry."

"Callaway was protesting too much." It was Byatt, the surgeon, who chipped in with this. "Wasn't that what you felt, Elrick?"

Elrick nodded. "It was one of the possibilities. Bluster is a fairly standard response in the sort of situation I've been sketching. But Callaway's bewilderment and indignation were extraordinarily convincing."

"But surely," I said, "the fact of his being an actor is pretty relevant there?"

And at this our junior member, John Appleby, broke in. As Appleby is high up at Scotland Yard, he is commonly listened to with respect on these occasions.

"My money's on that," he said. "Let's remember that Callaway is an actor."

"And quite able"—I drove this home— "to put over a turn even on an experienced lawyer like our host."

"Or was it—after all—the lady who had protested too much?" Byatt, with a chuckle that is characteristic of him, flew off at a tangent.

"Isn't a pretty creature—I think that's how Elrick described her—more likely to pull the wool over an intelligent lawyer's eyes than the cleverest actor is? Nothing seems likelier than that she was making up the whole story. Hence Callaway's reaction."

I found this rather steep. "Oh, come," I said, "Why ever should she do such a thing? Elrick is her husband's solicitor. He might have gone straight to the General. Surely she wouldn't risk that, simply for the sake of making herself interesting?"

"My dear chap"—Byatt turned to me tolerantly— "I see you don't know much about neurotic and hysterical women. The fantasies they'll spin about themselves—and swear to—have to be heard to be believed."

Appleby nodded. "I'm sure that's so," he said. "But have we had any evidence that Mrs. Dominey was either hysterical or neurotic?"

"She was neither." Elrick spoke decisively. "I repeat that she wasn't clever. She could easily be deceived, but she wasn't unbalanced.

"And now I expect you've all got as far as Appleby plainly has. The solution lay in the fact of Callaway's being an actor—and a character actor at that. Those admiring letters from Mrs. Dominey had never reached him. They had been intercepted by a smooth rascal called Lipsedge, who then had a job as his dresser."

"Lipsedge?" Appleby repeated. "I think I've heard of him."

"I expect you have. A smart crook. He realised that there need be no substantial physical resemblance between the figure Mrs. Dominey had admired across the footlights and the fellow who might walk out of the stage-door and claim to be the actor.

"So he impersonated his employer, rapidly got the lady into an awkward situation, and hoped to get away with a tidy sum in blackmail before the imposture was detected."

"And so it all ended happily?" Byatt asked.

"Except for Lipsedge—yes."

"And did you find it necessary to take General Dominey into your confidence?"

Elrick smiled. "That would be telling." he said.

WHO SUSPECTS THE POSTMAN?

WHO SUSPECTS THE POSTMAN?

PARTINGTON HOUSE presented a forlorn appearance as Appleby kicked the snow from his shoes and hurried in. The bleak thin light of a winter morning made the splendid rooms seem pretentious and uneasy, and the dismal effect was increased by the litter left over from the party of the night before. There were champagne glasses on the floor, and in the great green and gold drawing-room nobody had turned out the lights on the Christmas tree.

It had been very much a Christmas party. Lord Partington himself gave evidence of this when Appleby was ushered into his presence in the library. There was still a smear of red greasepaint high on one cheekbone. And—what made his appearance really fantastic—he had failed to remove two tufts of white cotton-wool from his eyebrows.

Lord Partington, clearly, had been representing Father Christmas. He did that at this fancy-dress party every year—making a spectacular appearance and disappearance, it was said, on a sledge, and presenting his guests with presents conceived on rather a lavish scale. Lord Partington, in fact, had a showy side. And this annual party, given not to children but to bored grown-ups, was an expression of it.

"It was enormously valuable, you know." Lord Partington began abruptly. "The Whang Vase, it's called. An ancestor brought it from Pekin. Pretty well stole it, I dare say."

Appleby nodded. "And now it has been stolen from you?"

"Yes—during my party. And when I wasn't three paces from it, if you ask me. You saw that Christmas tree? The Whang Vase stood in an alcove just beside it. It's a large pot-bellied affair about three feet high. I can't say I ever saw much in it myself. But it's enormously valuable, as I say."

"But surely. Lord Partington, it could hardly be worth much to a thief? It he tried to dispose of it, it would be identified at once?"

"That's the deuce of it, my dear fellow. Those affairs go, it seems, in pairs. Somewhere in the world there's a missing Whang Vase, identical with mine. So it's open to anybody who gets hold of mine to invent some cock-and-bull story about having picked it up in a junk shop."

"And when," Appleby asked, "was the disappearance discovered?"

"Quite late, when most of my guests had left. I must say your people were here in no time. They'll have told you how the thing was done?"

Appleby nodded. "I gather that your butler found a window open on a staircase at the back of the house, and a rope trailing down from it into a yard. It seems an odd way to make off with a large fragile object."

"Quite so." Lord Partington nervously lit a cigarette. "But nobody, you see, could have walked out of the front door with that great thing without being spotted by half-a-dozen servants. And the same goes for any route through the kitchens and so forth. But once down that rope and into the yard, the fellow could get away easily."

"I see. Well. I think I'll have a look at that window."

It was twenty minutes before Appleby returned to the library. "I'm afraid," he said, "that I must ask some questions about your guests."

Lord Partington was startled. "My guests? You think one of them made off down that rope?"

"I don't think that anybody did. The rope is a mere false trail. And whoever arranged it didn't reckon with the snow. There's an untrodden carpet of it in that yard. So that's that."

"But suspecting my guests just doesn't make sense. None of them could have got away with it."

"That may be so." Appleby paused for a moment. "But a few of them, at least, must be thoroughly familiar with your house?"

"Certainly."

"Then one of them may simply have hidden the thing until he—or she—can collect it on a favourable occasion. There must, after all, be a hundred hiding places in a great mansion like this."

Lord Partington stood up abruptly. "I can't believe it," he said. "That it should still be here isn't a possible solution at all."

It was only after close questioning that Lord Partington let slip the rather special position of his old friend Colonel Wain, who was an authority on Chinese pottery, with connections among collectors in many parts of the world. But Wain had never been a man of wealth. And now, Lord Partington believed, he was having difficulty in making both ends meet. "But that, you know," he said drily to Appleby, "doesn't necessarily make him a thief."

"Of course it doesn't. But we must keep an eye on him, all the same. Do you remember when he left your party? No? He wasn't conspicuous? What sort of costume did he come in to this fancy dress affair of yours?"

For a second Lord Partington hesitated. "I don't remember," he said.

Appleby found Colonel Wain in his flat off Piccadilly. He was an elderly hard-bitten man with keen grey eyes. Appleby was a little startled to find him sitting in the company of the Home Secretary. "You've come about this theft?" Wain asked.

"Yes, Colonel. But I mustn't disturb you when you are with Mr. Mellanby."

"Never mind Mellanby." Wain barked this out. "He and I are old friends. Go ahead. What do you want to know?"

"I want to know in what costume you went to Lord Partington's last night."

There was a silence—and then Wain gave an odd sigh. "I went as a postman," he said. "And you'll be quite right if you suppose that part of the outfit consisted of a large sack." He turned to Mellanby. "What do you think, Jim?"

"That you'd better tell the truth. Or shall I do it for you?"

"Please do." Wain looked curiously aged and broken. "I never thought it would come to this."

"The colonel and I left Partington's affair together." Mellanby was accustomed to waste no words. "And in our taxi he asked me to search that postman's bag. It contained empty cardboard boxes—nothing else. Can you take my word for that?"

Appleby smiled. "Yes, Minister. I think I can." He turned to Wain. "Just what had Lord Partington done?"

"He took advantage of some distraction to slip *his* bag—Father Christmas's, you know—over the Vase. And then he gathered it up and had himself drawn out of the drawing-room on his ridiculous sledge. I was the only man who spotted the manoeuvre—in the East, you know, one gets into the way of keeping one's eyes open—and I was absolutely astounded. Then I remembered that Partington had made a great point of my coming as a postman, bag and all. It was a plot against me." Wain's voice faltered. "And he is one of my oldest companions."

"It was certainly a plot, sir. He arranged a very palpable false trail with a rope from a window, such as a not-too-clever guest might have contrived in order to suggest an outside job. And then, in talking to me, he managed to bring you, Colonel, into the picture in a thoroughly suspicious way. Nothing could ever be proved against you, of course. But, having left Partington House with that bulky bag, you would be a suspect to point to when the matter was being investigated by the insurance people."

Wain nodded slowly. "And that is what it was about?"

"Certainly, Lord Partington stole his own Whang Vase in order to collect the insurance on it, and subsequently to sell it quietly as the twin of the one that had ostensibly been stolen from him. There would be a double profit."

Mellanby stood up. "And Partington?" he asked. "Will he ever be more than a suspect?"

Appleby shook his head. "I'm afraid not, Minister. The first move we make will alarm him, and the vase will just unobtrusively turn up in Partington House again. A bad business."

Mellanby nodded, and turned to Wain. "A bad business, indeed. We can't even throw him out of the club."

Wain looked at his friend in somber dismay. "Yet, one couldn't belong to the same club as a fellow like that. We'll have to resign ourselves."

Appleby looked at the two perturbed gentlemen. "At least," he said, "a reflection of general usefulness emerges. One doesn't necessarily get away with a thing even when one is quite sure one has it in the bag."

A CHANGE OF FACE

A CHANGE OF FACE

"EVERY BRANCH of the medical profession," Byatt told the Mystery Club, "has its own peculiar ethical problems. Elrick must be aware of a good many of them."

The lawyer nodded. "Mostly problems of confidence, aren't they? But others as well."

"Certainly others as well. And my own job, which is that of plastic surgeon, produces some queer ones. Most of my time, of course, goes to straight-forward work repairing the effects of accident and injury. But there is what's popularly called the cosmetic side. Some chaps simply run a high-powered beauty parlour. Well, good luck to them. You can genuinely promote a woman's well-being, no doubt, just by doing something about the shape of her nose. That sort of thing happens never to have been a great line of my own. Last summer, however, I was asked to do something about a nose—and well-being certainly came in."

"A woman's well-being?" Elrick asked.

"No. A nation's. Or that was the story."

We all looked at the surgeon in surprise. "I imagine," John Appleby said, "that this wasn't very near home?"

"It was in Ruritania. I'll call the country that, because the name gives you most of the relevant associations. Only this Ruritania is a republic—or *was* a republic when I arrived there on holiday. I believe I was the last foreigner allowed in for quite a time. There were three important parties: the national democrats, the democratic nationalists, and the monarchists. And it wasn't quite clear whether the national democrats or the democratic nationalists were in power. What was quite unmistakable was how much they hated each other.

"At first I found it merely amusing. In Zigzag, the capital, people were marching about in ragged processions all day. There were proclamations and strikes and rallies all tumbling on top of each other; and it was possible to see the whole thing in a comic-opera light. But not for long. At bottom of course, it was no laughing matter. I dare say some of you know the sort of thing, and the kind of sights that get one down."

"Quite so." Warriner, who is in the Foreign Service, spoke from the bottom of the table. "Kids wandering round because their parents and uncles and aunts are all in quod. Public services collapsing. Babies getting themselves born in queues outside the hospitals, while loud speakers bellow political eloquence overhead. Haven't I seen it."

Byatt poured himself out a glass of port.

"I had a talk with our *chargé d'affaires* and it was his opinion—quite off the record—that the country's best hope lay in a restoration of the monarchy. The pretender to the throne was a young man called Prince Igor, who had lived in exile since early boyhood, being educated in complete retirement. Hardly anybody had ever set eyes on him, but he was known to be a civilised sort of lad, with some sensible ideas. Where Prince Igor was at the moment, nobody could tell. But there was a rumour that his supporters were preparing some sort of coup.

"All this was interesting, but no affair of mine. Or so I thought until, a couple of nights later, I was visited secretly in my hotel by a wholly surprising personage. He arrived in a hat and overcoat so shabby that he had difficulty in getting in. But once safely in my room he threw these off, and I saw a venerable aristocrat with exquisitely groomed silver hair—and round his neck a really startling gold chain. He pointed to this and introduced himself as Count X, High Chamberlain to the country's lawful monarch, King Igor the Fifteenth."

Byatt paused on this, and I couldn't help laughing. "My dear chap," I asked, "wasn't that very much the idea?"

"Count X," Appleby added, "having an eye on your professional services?"

Byatt smiled cheerfully. "Just that," he said. "We'll say that the count's story quite fired my imagination. Whether it altogether satisfied my intellect is another matter."

"I began," he went on, "by mentioning medical ethics. Whether what I agreed to do squared with them, I really don't know.

"Well, what Count X told me was this. His royal master was in Zigzag at the moment, prepared to place himself at the head of his supporters and put both the national democrats and the democratic nationalists in their place.

"That didn't mean, apparently, in gaol, for this amiable young prince was full of the most liberal convictions. I felt prepared to wish him well. And I was quite distressed when I heard about the snag."

"The snag?" Elrick asked.

"Prince Igor had already made one bid for the throne—and it had gone hopelessly wrong. A year before, he had entered the country under the name of Colonel N, and led a monarchist uprising under that discreet *nom de guerre*. It had been a disastrous failure. His followers had done some rash and indiscriminate shooting; and Colonel N, whose appearance had become well known in Zigzag, was so universally execrated that Prince Igor—who was supposed, of course, to be still in exile—had to disown him. But as soon as the prince presented himself in his own person now he would at once be recognized—as Colonel N. And his supporters, sounding opinion in Zigzag, concluded that the old feeling against Colonel N was still so strong that this recognition of his identity would be fatal to the prince's cause. But the appearance of the *prince*, remember, was still virtually unknown in his country. Hence the proposal that Count X put to me. I was to operate upon the young man so that he would no longer look in the least as the ill-fated Colonel N had looked."

"And you agreed?" Elrick asked.

"I did. It can't be said that I wholly believed the story—although I'm sure that I'd have liked to. And part of the attraction of the job lay in the fact that the technical difficulties looked like being considerable. But I satisfied myself that Count X had adequate facilities available in an obscure nursing home in a Zigzag suburb.

"I was received there in rather comical state by two more aristocratic-looking persons, who conducted me into a sort of improvised throne-room, dominated by an oil-painting of the Prince's grandfather, King Igor the Thirteenth. He was a massively bearded figure, and the beard worried me. It plucked, so to speak, at some recollection I just couldn't fix, but which I felt to be relevant to my present enterprise. And then the young man came in and received me very graciously. He wasn't, as a matter of fact, quite so young as I expected. But he certainly had a nose with which quite a lot could be done. And I did it. Within a month my work was done and I left the country.

"Count X presented me with a respectable cheque on a London bank. And he assured me that when his majesty was happily restored. I should immediately receive the Order of the Chimera, Second Class."

Warriner was amused at this. "But you never did?"

"No. And the monarchist coup just didn't happen. I must admit that I wasn't greatly surprised. And now, I dare say, some of you have tumbled to something like the truth of the matter?"

There was a short silence, and then Appleby spoke. "I think you said something about a beard?"

"Exactly. What had eluded my recollection was this: Prince Igor's grandfather, like many of his line, was a haemophiliac. He wore a beard because a single cut shaving would have been a very dangerous accident. His grandson would almost certainly have inherited the trouble—which meant that my operation ought infallibly to have killed him."

"In fact, it wasn't Prince Igor you operated on at all?"

"It decidedly was not. I met Count X a couple of months ago in New York—not looking nearly so aristocratic. He was kind enough to thank me for helping to get the fugitive democratic-nationalist leader, Krambec, safely out of the country.

"After my attentions Krambec had got across the frontier without attracting the slightest suspicion. And he had nothing to fear in the way of subsequent attempts at assassination, since none of his enemies could recognize him."

Byatt reached again for the decanter. "My story has its humiliating side. X and his friends clearly reckoned that I'd fall much more readily for a prince than a politician. So they put, you might say, a romantic face on the matter."

THE THEFT OF THE
DOWNING STREET LETTER

THE THEFT OF THE DOWNING STREET LETTER

T HIS STORY," I told my fellow-members of the Mystery Club, "isn't a true story. Quite frankly, I'm making it up."

"Fair enough," Sir John Appleby said. "One can't expect an industrious romancer to have much time for the merely factual. Go ahead."

"Indeed," I went on, "it's scarcely a story at all. It's *about* a story. Or better, it's about the ethics of a story."

"The ethics of a story?" Byatt, the surgeon, looked at me dubiously through a wreath of cigar smoke. "Do detective stories, and so forth, have ethics? They seem to me to be mostly about a disastrous lack of them."

"Not at all," I replied stiffly. "A little time ago, you were talking about every branch of the medical profession having its own ethical problems. Well, it's the same with the craft of fiction. The greatest writers, dealing with the deepest matters, have always to consider whether they are playing fair—to their characters, to the truth of their own imagination to the universe as they conceive the universe to be. And it's the same with the humblest sort of writing. There's always a need to play fair. The reader is judge and jury, and he's entitled to all the evidence."

This metaphor naturally prompted our lawyer to chip in.

"You mean," Elrick asked, "not suppressing clues, and that sort of thing?"

"Just that. Or making the clues adequate clues. If they are too obvious, you insult the intelligence of your reader. If they are too tenuous, he may feel cheated and want his money back."

Byatt chuckled. "He won't get it."

"Or he may feel he wants his *time* back, which is worse. So it's up to the conscientious writer to do his best—and I assure you he commonly does." I asserted this with modest firmness.

"And now, I'll tell you about Katkin and his letter. And about Serracino and his flat."

"Katkin?" Byatt asked.

"Katkin is the head of a foreign government." I paused. "But I think I'll tell you about Serracino first. That will be fairer. And this is all a matter of fairness, as I've said. Notice the chap's name, to begin with. Serracino. It's thoroughly exotic, which is a strong hint that he's a bad hat. His manners are displeasing, too, and his taste is execrable. For instance, there's this flat I mentioned. I quite spread myself in describing the living-room. It's the sort of place in which liqueur bottles have been turned into lamp-stands and ash-trays are offered you by bronze nudes, and cigarette-lighters lurk in small suits of armour, and papier-mâché galleons stand on chests displaying dates like '1564' or '1066,' and the curtains—"

"Yes, yes," Byatt interrupted. "We see the room. *Avanti.*"

"But Serracino shows some signs of serious pursuits. Photography, for instance. And he is something of a reader. There are lots of books in that showy room, including a remarkable collection of detective stories from Edgar Allan Poe and Conan Doyle down to the present day. Well, that's Serracino. Now I can go back to Katkin."

Byatt shook his head. "I don't think," he said, "that this is going to be at all a well-constructed story. But go on. Katkin is the head of a foreign government."

"Just that. And he writes a letter to the Prime Minister, Lord Auldearn. I know that Prime Ministers aren't often in the Lords nowadays, but I think it's still a convention valuable for giving a story tone. Well, Katkin's letter to Lord Auldearn is stolen. That's what my story is about. It's a missing-letter story."

Elrick, who was our host, at this point passed the brandy. "A very reliable kind," he murmured, ambiguously. "Proceed."

"The letter is stolen," I repeated. "And somebody very important at Scotland Yard is called in to recover it. He might be Appleby. In fact, I'll call him Appleby—just among ourselves."

Appleby reached for the decanter. "Thank you very much," he said. "I hope I don't fall down on the job."

"I think you're not going to do too badly. And now, let me describe the letter, and explain the circumstances of the theft. The letter isn't very long, but it's terribly important. And it's a handsome affair. You couldn't tuck it away just anywhere. Katkin, having risen from humble circumstances to the position of a virtual dictator, delights in his command of all the best materials. You can almost guess that his pen—which has been made in America—is solid gold; and you can see that he writes on a handsome sort of bogus vellum in bold black ink. Of course, you can't—"

Byatt looked up from his rummer. "Who's 'you'?" he demanded.

"Anybody. You must understand that my story isn't yet quite in the *form* of a story—"

"Oh—very well. Go on."

"Of course you can't *read* the letter, because it's in Katkin's own language and queer alphabet. But—"

Byatt interrupted again. "Is this chap a Russian?"

"I don't say. It's often more effective not to be quite explicit about these points."

"Is it? I shouldn't have thought so. But continue."

I was conscious of breathing rather hard. "Very well," I said. "I *will* continue. The circumstances in which Katkin's letter is stolen aren't important, but they can probably be worked up into something quite amusing in itself—rather comical cabinet ministers and senior officials, and a light handling of the theme of dismay in high places. You know the sort of thing."

Byatt nodded. "We do," he said with emphasis.

"Appleby is swiftly on the scent. And after one or two false casts, his suspicion comes to rest on Serracino. Although Serracino, as I've explained, is rather a low, flashy person, he has in some mysterious way had the opportunity to filch Katkin's vitally important letter from Lord Auldearn's desk. Appleby is pretty well certain of his quarry. Serracino's flat is watched. His telephone is tapped. He is overheard ringing up a surgeon."

Byatt was startled. "A surgeon?"

"An unsuccessful and drunken surgeon called Burge, now well known to the police as being in the pay of a foreign power."

"I see." Byatt took this soberly.

"What Serracino is heard saying to Burge is that he is holding something rather interesting, and that perhaps Burge might care to call. That is enough for Appleby. He obtains a search-warrant and raids Serracino's flat."

"Does the Prime Minister," Elrick inquired curiously, "go along, too?"

"No. He sits in suspense at No. 10.

"Well, there is nothing found on Serracino's person. So Appleby and his assistants begin a minute search of the flat. They are, as you may imagine, extremely skilled at the job. But they find nothing. The reader is now in suspense, too. Or he ought to be."

"My dear fellow." Byatt murmured. "I feel my own pulse pounding at this moment. Continue, I beg."

"Appleby and his men hunt and hunt. But nothing is found. And all the time Appleby is haunted by the feeling that he has *seen* something that is pointing him straight at the truth. He has seen it, but he can't quite fix it. You know the notion? I've worked it before."

Byatt—rather disagreeably, I felt—gave a hollow groan.

"And that's all," I said rather abruptly. "Have I afforded a decent clue?"

There was a blank silence. Then Elrick spoke in his dry solicitor's way.

"Didn't you say something about photography? Perhaps Serracino had got Katkin's letter on to a tiny scrap of microfilm, and then destroyed the original?" I shook my head.

"Poe." It was Appleby—the real Appleby—who spoke. Your precious detective had Poe's Purloined Letter knocking at his thick skull—the letter that couldn't be seen just because it was so utterly obviously displayed."

"Exactly!" I looked at Appleby with considerable affection. "And when my man tumbled to that, how did it lead him straight to Katkin's letter?"

Appleby shook his head. "I haven't"—he said—"a clue."

I looked at the others in despair. Their faces were completely vacant.

"But the room!" I cried. "Don't you remember what kind, of room it was? Try to imagine the lamp-shades!"

"Lamp-shades?" Appleby shook his head. I thought I had never seen a man look so singularly idiotic.

"Made out of old parchment or vellum documents: wills, leases, indentures—any old thing. You *must* have seen them! And Serracino had simply pasted—"

"Yes, of course." It was Elrick, our host, who broke in briskly. "Jolly good. *Jolly* good—eh? Stupid of us. Capital story it will make—really *capital*. Now will somebody spin that brandy?"

THE TINTED DIAMONDS

THE TINTED DIAMONDS

APPLEBY PREFACED his story by handing round what in court would be called an exhibit. It was a photograph—of the largest size one commonly meets with—of an elderly lady in evening dress. She had a tiara and diamonds and an ostrich-feather fan.

It seemed to me that one might have come upon her on the front page of any journal devoted to fashionable and semi-fashionable tattle.

"Was she murdered?" I asked hopefully.

"Dear me, no. Her misfortune wasn't of quite that extremity." Appleby glanced round the other members of the Mystery Club. "Anybody know her?"

Plumbridge, who divides women into those he has painted and those he has not, was the first to respond.

"Never set eyes on her," he said. "Wife of a civic dignitary in the Midlands somewhere, I'd guess."

Byatt laughed at this.

Warriner took another glance at the photograph. "It's Angela Jeff," he murmured.

And of course Lady Angela Jeff it was. But Plumbridge was determined not to be impressed.

"Ah, yes. The daughter of some obscure earl, who married in Mr. Jeff somebody obscurer still. And certainly there seems nothing out-of-the-way about her."

"Nor about her photograph?" Appleby said.

"Absolutely not."

Appleby was delighted. "Quite so," he said. "And there's the rub."

"I can imagine her as painted by Plumbridge," I said. "A frankly cosmetic surface, surrounding faded blue eyes."

"And her hair." Appleby asked, "—would that be blue too?"

"Of course not." I checked myself. "But yes—of course. That sort of blue-tinted wash that has been all the go among ladies of a certain age."

"Precisely. Lady Angela went in for that blue tint in rather a big way. Having decided that her hair was a success—"Appleby broke off. "But I'm not telling this story very well. Of course, it's more difficult than any of *your* stories. Because of its being scientific, you know."

"What do you mean—scientific?" I asked.

"Well, all your stories, although highly diverting, have been pretty well out of the ark. They've all happened within the last twelve months but they *might* have happened at any time during the last 50 years. Not so with Lady Angela. She is extremely up to date. Having decided to favour blue hair, she proceeded to elect blue diamonds as well." Appleby tapped the photograph. "Those *are* blue."

Lady Angela was certainly wearing what appeared to be a striking necklace of diamonds. But none of us was very impressed. "There's nothing particularly up-to-date about blue diamonds." Warriner said, "I can remember my mother—"

"No doubt." Appleby cut this interpolation short.

"Blue diamonds have always come from time to time from the mines. But this is a matter of artificial tinting Lady Angela decided to have her diamonds tinted. And there was nothing to stop her. It's something that has become feasible just within the last few months. The atomic research people will do it for you."

"Is it commercially advantageous?" Plumbridge asked.

"That's debatable. But the diamonds were Lady Angela's absolute property, to do what she liked with. Her husband the obscure Mr. Jeff, had very little influence with her. In point of fact, he was something of an adventurer, and her marriage to him—late in life—had proved to be socially rather an embarrassment.

"I ought to mention that although the lady had no children by Jeff, there was in fact a daughter by a previous marriage. And her first husband, it seems, had no great confidence in her sagacity for he left the child's affairs entirely in the hands of his solicitor, a shrewd old person called Closs.

"Closs did his best to keep on good terms with Lady Angela since she had a substantial private fortune—including her diamonds—which he hoped to see go eventually to the daughter. At the same time, Closs was disposed—as you may well imagine—to keep a pretty sharp eye on the Jeff *ménage*."

Appleby paused to light his pipe, and Byatt offered a comment. "The watchful Closs didn't take to the idea of letting the atom-busting chaps have their fun with the family diamonds?"

"He didn't like it a bit. But when he tried to enlist the support—for what it was worth—of the inconsiderable Jeff, he got himself roundly snubbed. Jeff thought that his aristocratic wife would look wonderful in blue diamonds. He even made an uneasy joke about their matching her blue blood. Some time later, he heard that the transmutation—or whatever is the correct word for it—had taken place. So when he met Jeff one afternoon in a club, he decided to mention the matter again in a spirit of accommodation. I mean that Closs thought it would be diplomatic not to appear to cut up rusty over spilt milk. He said he believed Lady Angela looked charming in her transformed jewels and he hoped he might have the pleasure of seeing her in them one day.

"And now I must tell you how I entered the affair myself. It was again a matter of a meeting in a club. Closs—whom I've known slightly for many years—passed across a weekly paper to me. What I saw was a reproduction of *this*"—and Appleby again tapped the photograph—"and when he gathered that I knew nothing about Lady Angela or her husband he told me the facts of the case much as I've told them to you now.

"He hadn't, he confessed, much rational cause for being annoyed. Whether or not the diamonds had dropped in value as a result of their adventure was something he had taken expert advice on, and it seemed to be an open question. Moreover, Lady Angela was on perfectly good terms both with her daughter and with Closs himself. But it just *did* vex him to see her posing there, with her blue hair and her freshly transformed jewels. He could almost imagine the damned thing as it would look he said if it was two-pence coloured.

"I had another glance at the photograph and I asked Closs if he was certain it had been taken *after* the stones had been turned blue. He replied rather testily, that there was no question of it. Lady Angela herself had described to him how her first action on getting the things back from the laboratory had been to dress up and summon a photographer."

Appleby paused for a moment. "And at that, of course. I suggested to Closs that we had better set about having the obscure Jeff put inside."

"Inside?" Byatt asked blankly

"In quod. Jeff had been regressing."

Perhaps because we were an elderly lot and indeed only fit for the ark, we merely stared at Appleby.

"What was wrong with the photograph," he said, "was precisely that there was *nothing* wrong with it. The residual radio-activity in treated diamonds would be very slight. But it would be sufficient, after that short interval of time to produce an unmistakable fuzz upon a photographic plate. In Lady Angela's photograph every detail was entirely clear-cut. We could be quite certain, then, that although the necklace in which Lady Angela had been photographed might have been blue, it had never been inside that laboratory.

"And what had happened soon became clear. Jeff had seized upon his wife's fancy in order to do himself quite a bit of good. He had offered to arrange the whole matter, had taken away the diamonds, and simply had them copied in blue paste. He trusted to Lady Angela's naïve delight in her new toys to blind her to the fact that in an unsuspected sense, they were no longer as they had been."

There was a pause.

"And *was* Jeff put inside?" Byatt asked.

Appleby smiled. "Dear me, no. In a family, little matters of that sort have to be—well, composed. But Lady Angela now has her real diamonds again."

JERRY DOES A GOOD TURN
FOR THE DJAM

JERRY DOES A GOOD TURN
FOR THE DJAM

"CRIMINAL INVESTIGATION," Detective-Inspector Sir John Appleby said, "is commonly an unsatisfactory pursuit for the moralist. The detective solves his problem, in the sense that he determines the true facts of the case. But the moral implications may remain very confused, so that no useful conclusion can be drawn."

"Useful for what?" I asked.

"Useful as a guide to conduct." Appleby seemed to speak quite seriously. "The tale inclines to end, that is to say, without a moral. But of course it isn't always so. For instance, there was the unfortunate affair of Smith. Some precept or axiom could be extracted from that. You remember Smith?"

"Spotty Smith, who became a professor somewhere?"

"No, not Spotty. I should imagine Spotty's life to have been entirely blameless and uneventful."

"Then you mean Basil Smith, who certainly left off being blameless pretty early. It was remarkable he wasn't sacked. As it was, he gave bird-watching a very bad name in the school."

"No, not Basil Smith either. I'm thinking of Jerry Smith. But you mayn't remember him."

"Not remember Jerry!" I roared with laughter. "The boy who called up half a dozen fire brigades and then let off the smoke bomb in the library? Of course I remember him. And I believe he brought off something similar when he went to Cambridge. But I never heard anything of him after that."

Appleby smiled a shade grimly. "I can tell you something," he said.

"I was walking up Whitehall one morning," Appleby began, "when a car drew up to the kerb and its occupant threw open a

111

door and hailed me. I recognised my old friend Oliphant of the Foreign Office. He was in a great state of excitement. 'Appleby,' he cried, 'you're just the man. When in doubt, always nab a bobby. Jump in.'

"Well, I jumped in for I could trust Oliphant not to be wasting my time on a mere whim. 'It's the Djam of Dongo,' he said, as the car shot off again towards Trafalgar Square. 'He flew in, utterly unexpectedly a couple of hours ago. Now he's at the Picardy, and proposing to hold a press conference any minute. It's most disturbing.'

" 'But why ever shouldn't he?' I asked. For I was entirely vague about the Djam, knowing only that he was some sort of picturesque Eastern potentate.

"Oliphant shook his head. 'I can't think what's come over him. Of course, he's in Europe a great deal. He likes it. But he manages to square his trips with a very strict seclusion. They say it's some-thing to do with his religion.' And Oliphant laughed nervously.

" 'And isn't it?' I asked.

" 'My dear Appleby, there's an utterly fanatical sect out for his blood. The most elaborate arrangements have to be made when he moves from one country to another. Yet here he is, simply drop-ping in out of the blue, and proposing to expose himself to all and sundry in a large hotel. . . . Thank heaven, here we are.'

"We had been bowling along the Strand, and now we had swung into the courtyard of the Picardy. Our chauffeur had clearly been told to hurry. But he was being reasonably careful, all the same—which was the only reason that we didn't collide with an ambulance coming the other way. It went off with its bell clang-ing. And Oliphant was positively pale where he sat. 'By God,' he said, '—what if they've got him?' "

Appleby had paused, so that I looked at him expectantly. "And they had?" I asked.

Appleby nodded. "To put it briefly, the bullet had found its billet—and at the very moment the Press conference was getting under way. So the whole place was in desperate confusion; reporters and photographers jumping into cars or shouting for taxis or scrumming for telephones, and policemen lumbering up from all over the place. Nobody seemed to know whether the Djam was dead, or dying, or just rather nastily wounded. And as soon as he had been got off to hospital it was discovered that his *entourage* had bolted."

I laughed at this. "I don't know that I blame them. I suppose they were countrymen of the Djam's?"

"Three coffee-coloured gentlemen in flowing white robes. And they'd simply gone to earth before anybody could stop them. As for the assailant, he seemed to have got clean away too. The shot had come from the back of the room, and we could find nobody who could give the slightest help about it. We spent nearly an hour doing what we could. When we left the hotel for the hospital the posters were already out. REIGNING PRINCE SHOT IN LONDON. Oliphant swore at them softly as we drove across Westminster Bridge."

"And did the Djam turn out to be dead?"

Appleby chuckled. "We proved to have no means of telling. He had vanished."

"Vanished!"

"You may well sound surprised. There was a general air of its being the most incredible thing ever to have happened in a great London hospital. He'd been left on one of those sinister trolley affairs for about ten seconds, with nobody in the room except a junior nurse. And a couple of confident-looking fellows in white coats had simply come and wheeled him away. The trolley was found later in a lobby. And there was another rather dramatic discovery as well. It looked as if the Djam had regained consciousness and tried to leave a message. A fountain pen and a crumpled piece of paper were found tossed into a corner."

"He'd managed to write something?"

"No more than what looked like the beginning of the word '*help.*'"

"There wasn't much sense in that."

"We supposed that he was thoroughly bemused, and was writing that when his captors pounced on him again. By the time Oliphant and I left the hospital there was a new lot of posters on the streets. HOSPITAL SENSATION SHOT PRINCE KIDNAPPED!"

"And was it all," I asked, "really so very serious? I mean diplomatically and so on?"

"My dear man, the papers next morning already carried reports of rioting in Dongo. By noon we knew there was a civil war. An hour or two later we heard that the police in Paris had arrested an impostor who was claiming to be the Djam alive and well. But it was a little later that the thing took a really grave turn. In one of the great chancelleries some genius had worked it out that the disappearance of the Djam was the first move in a war of aggression. The Russian government left Moscow. The American fleet was ordered to sea. There was even a rumour that somebody had pushed a button—perhaps the real button or perhaps one of the dummy ones. The world was on the brink of chaos."

Appleby was silent for a moment, and I said the obvious thing. "It can't have gone over—or I'd have noticed."

"Quite so. There was, you see, that fountain pen. It proved, one may say, to be mightier than the sword."

"The pen was your only clue?" I asked.

"Yes. And the queer thing is that, in a sense. I recognised it from the first. I simply *knew,* that's to say, that it told me something. It had been chewed to a quite extraordinary degree. Now, many people chew pencils. But to chew at a fountain pen so that—"

I gave a shout of enlightenment. "Jerry Smith!"

"Exactly. That obstinate habit of his eventually came to me like a flash. Of course it was a very long shot. But I set about tracing him and found him in bed, being nursed by three justifiably scared cronies. His wound wasn't terribly serious, and one of the three happened to be a doctor, so they had a good chance of getting away with it."

"The thing had been planned as his biggest practical joke?"

"Just that. But he hadn't reckoned with that sect which was out for the Djam's blood. The plan was to hold the press conference and then vanish. Of course it was the real Djam who had the misfortune to get himself arrested in Paris."

"I see. But what happened at the hospital?"

"The cronies had bolted to their car, and later they followed the ambulance—changing themselves from coffee-coloured to white as they went along. Then a couple of them cleverly adapted their robes to impersonate hospital orderlies. That's how they got Jerry away. The scrawled message was simply designed to obscure the trail."

"And the Russian government." I asked rather drily, "returned to Moscow?"

"Certainly. And the American fleet went back to port. Can I get you a drink?"

I looked at Appleby suspiciously. "I think you said that this was an affair with a moral?"

"Indeed it is. Don't perpetrate a 1907 joke in a 1957 world."

THE LEFT-HANDED BARBER

THE LEFT-HANDED BARBER

"Y WIFE'S mother," Plumbridge said, "is the sort of woman who is constantly finding herself in the possession of treasures. And my story starts from that."

"Treasures?" I asked. "Do you mean domestics—the utterly unobtrusive parlour-maid and the wholly reliable cook?"

Plumbridge shook his head. "Not at all. I speak literally. But perhaps I ought to say that the good soul constantly *believes* herself to be finding treasures. Sometimes there's something in it, and sometimes there isn't.

"She has inherited, you see, a large house absolutely crammed with junk. Collecting—or rather sheer acquisitiveness—ran in her husband's family for generations. And now all the stuff is hers. She is spending her latter years very happily, exploring her riches—cupboard by cupboard and room by room. Elrick knows about her I think. He's her lawyer."

The solicitor nodded. "I certainly know your mother-in-law. When her discoveries are in the nature of old documents, she always brings them along to me. I rather think she hopes to find herself one day in possession of the title-deeds of the British Museum or the Albert Hall. But nothing very remarkable has turned up so far. She tells me, however, that it has been different in the field of art."

"And so it has," Plumbridge said. "There were real connoisseurs in the family at one time and another, and as a consequence we have had some genuine finds, I say 'we' because, when anything of the sort is in question, she always brings me in. If one's an artist, it's supposed one knows about art."

"And *do* you know about art?" Byatt, our surgeon, asked mildly.

Plumbridge cheerfully shook his head. "A popular portrait painter—Lord help him—hasn't much time to be an art historian.

But, of course, I have a notion of where to get an informed opinion. And that's what I set about doing when my wife's mother conceived herself to have discovered a Leonardo da Vinci."

"A Leonardo?" I said, rather startled. "You mean a painting?"

"No, no—simply a drawing. Even so it would be valuable if it could be proved authentic. So I decided to take this drawing along to Charles Tapsell."

"Ah—Tapsell." Byatt nodded with a great appearance of being well informed. "Almost a legendary figure. But elusive. You must have had the *entrée*, my dear fellow."

Plumbridge grinned, "Well, yes—I had. But it didn't last for long. I was kicked out in no time."

"Then it wasn't a Leonardo?" Elrick asked.

"You're quite right. It wasn't. But it couldn't be said I was making an absolute fool of myself. The subject was a favourite one with Leonardo—a Leda, as a matter of fact, with a couple of babies hatching out of eggs. So it was quite confidently that I rang up Tapsell one evening. I found an odd set-up. Tapsell is, as Byatt says, elusive in his old age. He lives in a flat, with a single manservant called Gunton who is even more ancient than himself, and I doubt whether he ever stirs out of the place. He has, of course, his very valuable private collection. But it didn't appear to keep him very sweet-tempered. I had miscalculated the hour, and when Gunton showed me in, I found Tapsell sitting in a sort of dressing-room, being shaved by a professional barber. He seemed a harmless man, but he was a substitute for the one who came regularly, and Tapsell wasn't pleased with him. He told the fellow that his razor was as blunt as a spoon, and that if he didn't bring a better one next day he'd be fired."

"An unpromising situation." Elrick said. "But, after all, poor old Tapsell hadn't even had his coffee."

Plumbridge nodded. "Well, at least I didn't keep him from it long. He took a single glance at the drawing, and tossed it back to me. 'Leonardo?' he said 'Stuff and nonsense, man! Fiddlesticks! Just look at the hatching. Good day to you.' And out I went."

Plumbridge paused to pour himself a glass of port. "Well, now," he presently continued, "I must make clear what my story is really about. As I came away from Tapsell's I found myself groping after something odd I'd seen there. Moreover what I'd *seen* hitched on to something quite different that I'd *heard*. But all that came into my head was the name of Hogarth."

"Hogarth?" Byatt asked, "The painter?"

"Yes. I've always been fond of Hogarth both as painter and engraver, but there seemed no reason why he should bob up into my mind now. He certainly hadn't been mentioned, and I was pretty sure that there wasn't anything by him visible on Tapsell's walls. This strange little problem even distracted me from what Tapsell had said about my drawing, and it was only later in the day that I found myself chewing over that. About the hatching, you know."

"Didn't you," I asked, "say something about babies coming out of eggs? I suppose Tapsell meant that they weren't emerging in the proper Leonardo manner."

To my considerable discomfiture, Plumbridge received this with a roar of laughter.

"My dear chap," he said, "not *that* kind of hatching! Tapsell was referring to the fine parallel lines with which in a drawing an artist suggests his shadows. And I saw when I'd reflected on the matter, that the old boy had some right to be rather short with me I had been uncommonly forgetful. For Leonardo is famous as the greatest artist definitely known to have been entirely left-handed. And it's his hatching that reveals the fact. When I'd recalled this and taken another look at the drawing, my own technical knowledge was sufficient to tell me that it was certainly by a right-handed draughtsman."

There was a short silence "Most interesting." Byatt said "But I don't quite see where Hogarth comes in."

"Nor did I—until I woke up next morning. Then it came into my head like a flash. There's a well-known Hogarth engraving with a barber in it; it's in his series *Four Times of Day*. And the barber appears left-handed like Leonardo and—what is the odd thing—like the fellow who was shaving Tapsell. For *that*, of course, is what I'd noticed. So now I'd solved you see my whole little complex of unconscious associations."

"And that's all?" Elrick asked.

"Not at all. It so happened that I travelled up to town quite early that morning with a chap called Grimwood who is a professor of psychology. I told him the circumstances.

"And, when I'd finished, 'interesting' was the first word he uttered. 'Interesting', he said. 'Very interesting indeed. For you've seen, you know, something a good deal rarer than a dead donkey.'

"And then he looked at his watch. 'Getting on for your friend Tapsell's rather belated shaving time.' He said, 'I'd pay him another visit if I were you.'"

"So I did," he said. "I went straight along pausing only to pick up a policeman at a corner. We arrived just in time to nab that harmless barber as he was making off with some of Tapsell's best things. He'd persuaded Tapsell to send Gunton out on a fool's errand; and then he'd just tied poor old Tapsell up and helped himself. Once he'd contrived somehow to take the place of the regular and genuine barber, the thing was simplicity itself."

There was a moment's silence and then Appleby spoke for the first time.

"And what is rarer than a dead donkey," he asked, "is, in fact, a left-handed barber?"

Plumbridge nodded "That's what my friend Grimwood pointed out to me. In this country they simply don't happen. They'd be too dangerous—because of the way they'd knock up against the next fellow in the shop."

"But," I said, "it was different in the eighteenth century. Hogarth had observed one."

Plumbridge shook his head "Not a bit of it. Hogarth's engravings went straight on the copper. So in the print, you see every image was reversed." Plumbridge glanced from one to another of us. "Have any of you," he asked, "ever been shaved by a left-handed man?"

There was a thoughtful silence and then Elrick spoke. "Yes," he said. "But it was in Sicily."

THE PARTY THAT NEVER GOT GOING

THE PARTY THAT NEVER GOT GOING

I SCARCELY know Herbert Tarrant," Appleby explained to his wife as he drew up the car at the lakeside quay. "I've no more than a notion of how he comes by his considerable wealth. So this invitation to his party is odd. He heard that we were in this part of Italy, it seems, and rang up. Or rather his secretary rang up."

Judith Appleby looked across the lake. The light was fading; the water gleamed like pale satin; the island stood out in silhouette. "It's tiny," she said. "Just room for the villa and a garden."

"Yes—but Tarrant gathers a large house-party there at this time. Here's the launch—the white one."

In a moment they were gliding over the water. And simultaneously, as if they were looking into a mirror, an identical launch drew away from the island. "Smooth organization," Appleby said. "There's always a launch either waiting at, or making for, each terminus."

They were hospitably received on landing by Tarrant's secretary, a young man who introduced himself as Walter Pinner.

"Mr. Tarrant makes me do all his jobs," he said cheerfully. "Particularly about parties. Everything from summoning the guests to his overwhelming board to expostulating with the caterers afterwards. He's looking for you. Let's find him."

Pinner's tone had conveyed an attitude to his employer that was not particularly loyal or pleasing. What he had said, on the other hand, seemed to have been prompted by an impulse to apologise for the slightly graceless manner in which the Applebys, who were almost strangers, had been invited to call.

"There he is!" Pinner said suddenly.

They had reached the lower of the two terraces now lit by coloured lamps. Their host stood on the upper terrace with a group of guests. Herbert Tarrant was tall—but this didn't account,

Judith thought, for the impression of dominance he made on her. He possessed a dark complexion, and a smile that could only be described as of malign command.

The effect was instantly antipathetic. And yet Tarrant was being courteous to guests upon whom—it struck Judith—there was discernible an air of constraint. Perhaps Tarrant's house-party was newly assembled and not settling down well.

Pinner led the Applebys to a further flight of steps. But he paused to give some directions to a servant, and when they reached the upper terrace Tarrant had disappeared.

"Too bad," Pinner said. "Let me find you a drink, and then collar the old boy for you. Do you know some of this crowd? I expect you do. It's a party arranged too much on cosmopolitan principles for my taste. Martini or champagne?"

Pinner disappeared. Appleby looked round. The secretary was right in calling it a cosmopolitan affair. The English preponderated, but there were French, Germans, Italians and a few Americans. Perhaps they were in language difficulties. There was an undeniable uncomfortableness about the whole gathering.

Judith had just declared that she didn't know a soul, when an elderly man stepped backwards, bumped into her, and turned round in polite apology. And Appleby spoke at once. "Good evening, colonel," he said easily.

But the elderly man himself was far from at ease. With an awkwardness contrasting with his distinguished military bearing, he flushed, made a curt reply and moved away.

Judith was indignant. "How very rude!" she said.

"You mustn't blame poor Colonel Haines. It's just that I've had professional relations with him—and of a delicate kind. There are people it's tricky meeting again, you know—outside Scotland Yard . . . Good Lord!"

Appleby had broken off suddenly and now Judith followed his gaze. It was directed upon a handsome woman standing in isolation at the edge of the terrace. "Not somebody else," Judith asked jokingly, "known to the police?"

"Indeed, yes. It's Lady Parker. I certainly don't want to encounter *her*. Let's take a stroll round."

They walked along the terrace. "Old Charles Billington," Appleby murmured. "Prince Luigi Peselli. And Mrs. Van Gander . . . . There's more in this than meets—"

At this moment the lights on the terraces and in the villa all went out. Darkness descended upon—as presently hubbub arose among—the hospitable Herbert Tarrant's party. And then a pistol-shot rang out somewhere in the villa.

When the lights went on again Appleby made straight for the island's little landing-stage. It looked as if he had been forestalled. Pinner was standing there. "I've just sent the launch for the police," he said.

"You think it's something serious?" Appleby asked this absently, as if he were listening for something else. Night had fallen. But one could just see, although it was now far away, a faint white blob that was the launch making for the shore. One could hear the pulse of its engine. But this faded, and there was a moment of silence, broken only by a faint splashing, before the answering throb of the second, and approaching, launch was heard.

"Serious? I'm sure of it. There's something damned strange about my precious employer's party." Pinner's voice was sharp with anxiety. "But at least nobody can get away."

"I suppose not. Was it you who turned on the lights again?"

Pinner shook his head. "It must have been one of the servants. It looks as if somebody had just thrown out the main switch. A quick theft in the darkness perhaps."

"One doesn't," Appleby said drily, "fire a revolver to celebrate successful theft."

They returned to the terrace and met Judith. "John," she said quietly, "Mr. Tarrant has been killed."

Tarrant had, in fact, been shot in a room used as a study, and to which he must have withdrawn for some purpose just before the lights went out. And Appleby, having inspected the body, assembled the guests in an adjoining apartment.

"The police," he said, "will be here in a few minutes. I want to make it clear that I have something to tell them. A number of the dead man's guests—perhaps *all* the dead man's guests—possessed a motive for committing this crime."

There was silence. Nobody uttered a word of protest. And the only movement came from Lady Parker, who sank into a chair.

"I happen to have information—let me hasten to say confidential information—about a number of you. You are wealthy people who for one reason or another are vulnerable to blackmail.

"There is only one explanation of your being brought together here. Tarrant's house-party is a cruel joke. It is, in fact, a sort of rent audit. You all turn up, and you all buy a further year's immunity—each, no doubt, unbeknown to the others. Is this admitted and agreed?"

There was a moment's silence. And then Colonel Haines spoke. "Perfectly true about myself," he said gruffly. "But it never dawned on me about the others."

"Thank you. Mr. Pinner and I are now going to meet the police. Will the rest of you please remain? You may not be kept in acute suspense for long."

Appleby was as good as his word. In fifteen minutes he returned to the villa alone. "Mr. Pinner," he said, "is under arrest. And I understand that, when you have given your names and permanent addresses to the authorities here, this singularly infelicitous party will be at liberty to break up."

"You see," Appleby said to Judith afterwards, "it just didn't · make sense."

"Tarrant's inviting us?"

"Just that. Tarrant wasn't mad, and his diabolical sense of humour wouldn't stretch to asking me along."

Judith nodded. "You must know more about high-class blackmail than anyone in England."

"I even had a notion—as I told you—where Tarrant's money came from. Then it was suspicious that there was no real evidence that Tarrant *had* invited us—and suspicious again that there was that delay in managing to present us to him.

"When I spotted the nature of my company, I suspected that we had been asked because of what I'd at once *notice* and *know*, Because, in fact, of the line of investigation I'd at once open up for the Italian police. As soon as it was realized that Tarrant was surrounded by victims of his blackmail, his secretary would virtually be freed of suspicion."

"It still seems to me that you had rather a slender case."

"Pinner's conduct down at the landing-stage made me quite certain of him. He spoke of just having sent the launch for the police. But it was already quite far across the lake. And an innocent man wouldn't have lingered there for a minute under the circumstances. No, he had been doing something else as well. There was his booty to get safely off the island: the rent which Tarrant had been collecting from his victims."

"Pinner had a confederate?"

"Yes, a confederate who has confessed. He was in a rowing-boat—a *black* rowing-boat, which would be quite invisible. Actually, I believe I heard the faint splash of the oars."

THE MYSTERY OF PAUL'S 'POSTHUMOUS' PORTRAIT

THE MYSTERY OF PAUL'S 'POSTHUMOUS' PORTRAIT

"I ACCEPTED rather an odd commission some time ago," the painter Plumbridge remarked one evening when he and Appleby were dining with me. "A kind of posthumous portrait."

"Aren't these things terribly difficult?" I asked. "You're given a few photographs of the deceased person and expected to produce a work of art on the strength of them."

Plumbridge laughed. "That would be easy enough—if you can produce works of art at all. What's difficult is producing, on the strength of photographs, a likeness that will in the least satisfy your client. It's with a good deal of misgiving that one takes on such a job."

"But," Appleby said with a mild curiosity, "you *did* take it on—this one?"

"Well, yes. It rather intrigued me. I was asked to work not from photographs but from a living person."

I stared. "I thought you said—"

"Quite so. The portrait was to be of a certain Paul Rawdon, who is dead. He died in childhood, as a matter of fact—and in America, where he had been evacuated during the war. But there is a surviving twin sister, Veronica, who now lives with her mother here in London. Paul and Veronica, being of opposite sex, couldn't of course be identical twins. But in childhood they did happen to be each the exact image of the other. And it was this that gave Mrs. Rawdon her idea—rather a morbid one, you may judge it."

"You were asked," I said, "to paint Paul as he would have been had he grown up, using the grown-up Veronica as your model?"

"Precisely," Plumbridge said.

Appleby, who was taking only a lazy interest in Plumbridge's story, looked up from lighting a cigar. "It was your job, so to speak, to masculine Veronica!"

"What a dreadful word! But it was just that. And it hasn't been easy. Veronica isn't at all mannish in appearance—and of course it wouldn't do to produce a Paul who was at all womanish. The difficulty of the commission was, in a sense, what made it respectable. There was a real problem—part intellectual and part aesthetic—involved. Still, I can't say I liked it, somehow. To take a girl into one's studio and paint an *imaginary* brother from her would be genuinely interesting and entirely harmless. But I wasn't doing exactly that."

I nodded. "You were claiming to be painting a potentially actual young man—who can't in fact be painted, because he didn't live beyond childhood. And that was uncomfortable."

"Something of the sort. And I was determined that, if the finished portrait was to go by the name of Paul Rawdon, it wouldn't be signed by Arthur Plumbridge. Perhaps it was fatuous of me, but I stipulated for that."

"Wasn't it," Appleby asked idly, "a pretty stiff stipulation? After all, you have a great name now, Plumbridge. Mrs. Rawdon might well feel that, in insisting on anonymity, you were rather doing her down."

Plumbridge shook his head. "No doubt it's mortifying to my vanity, but the plain fact is that Mrs. Rawdon didn't raise the slightest objection. She did, however, make two stipulations of her own. Paul, in his imaginary adulthood, was to be shown against an American background. I didn't demur, although it added to the spurious nature of the whole project. Clearly, if one once embarks on a rather unwholesomely sentimental project of this kind, one isn't entitled to boggle over details."

"What sort of a background did you provide?" I asked.

Plumbridge grinned rather maliciously. "I went the whole hog," he said, "and produced the skyline of New York. I couldn't have done Paul Rawdon more proud if he'd been the Queen Elizabeth or the Queen Mary."

Appleby's cigar was burning satisfactorily, and he now seemed to have more attention to give to Plumbridge's story. "What sort of people are these Rawdons?" he asked. "Prosperous, I suppose, to be able to commission the eminent Arthur Plumbridge to carry out their whim?"

"I don't know that they are." Plumbridge paused. "In fact, I've been a little worried. Mrs. Rawdon certainly isn't strikingly poor, but there's no sign of anything like wealth. In the end, as a matter of fact, I made the signature business an excuse for cutting my fee."

"Do you know any of their friends?"

"Absolutely not." Plumbridge frowned. "Well, that's not strictly accurate. I did see Mrs. Rawdon and Veronica one day driving with old Lady Trumper. You know her? They might have been going to a matinee."

Appleby nodded. "An eccentric old soul, and getting a bit doddery by now. But your client certainly has prosperous connections. Old Jane Trumper is worth the moon. By the way, you spoke of two stipulations by Mrs. Rawdon. What was the second?"

"It was a trifle odd. I had to undertake that the whole transaction should be on a strictly confidential basis, and that I should not retain any sketch or record of the portrait."

Appleby sat up—so that the first half-inch of ash fell from his cigar. "My dear chap," he said, "don't you recognize a high probability that you have involved yourself in a fraud."

"A fraud?" Plumbridge was startled. "However can that be?"

"I don't quite know. But, with your permission, I'll call on your sentimental client tomorrow morning."

It was about a week later that I ran into Appleby again. "Well," I asked, "how did you find Mrs. Rawdon and her Veronica?"

Appleby chuckled. "They haven't got away with it. I couldn't let them. It was really too much."

"There actually was a fraud?"

"Indeed there was. And yet, in the first instance, the deception might be called a pious one. Mrs. Rawdon was simply determined to spare dear Lady Trumper's feelings."

"Old Jane Trumper again! She is part of the story?"

"Decidedly. Paul and Veronica Rawdon were both her god-children, and she was devoted to them. Particularly to Paul. She prophesied brilliant things for them—and again particularly for Paul. Which was a pity. Because, soon after the children were evacuated to America, it became evident that Paul, although physically a really beautiful child, was mentally very much below par—and moreover deteriorating fast. I haven't got the medical details, but the sad fact is that he is still alive and in some sort of institution. And nobody has ever ventured to tell Lady Trumper the truth. First there was evasion, and then downright lies."

I was astonished. "Over that long period of years?"

"So it seems. When Paul didn't return to England with Veronica after the war, Lady Trumper was told some vague story of invalidism—invalidism of a sort that didn't detract from all the charm and promise she was imagining in the lad. Eventually he became an obsession with her, and all sorts of achievements had to be credited to him in order to keep her happy."

"But surely," I asked, "it was a very tall story—that a brilliant and successful youth suffered from some disability which prevented his crossing the Atlantic to visit his own home?"

Appleby nodded. "Certainly it was a tall story. In the cold light of reason there could be no sense to it. But you must consider this doting old woman's psychology. In her heart of hearts she must have known that she didn't want a flesh-and-blood godson, but only a dream one. So it was only intermittently that she allowed herself dimly to sense the queerness of the story. And meanwhile she had let it be known that she proposed to leave Paul a very large sum of money."

"It was at that point that Mrs. Rawdon's motive became definitely what you might call a corrupt one?"

"Yes. Lady Trumper's bequest would be perfectly legal, despite Paul's condition. And it would make a great difference to Mrs. Rawdon and Veronica as well. But Mrs. Rawdon was afraid that the foolish and pathetic old woman might be visited by some real gleam of doubt and uneasiness before she died. So she was going to have this overwhelming thing in reserve, a portrait of Paul, showing him to have grown up the very image of his sister, and declared to have been specially commissioned from an American painter as a present for his dear godmother."

"And having discovered the truth." I said, "you've told poor old Lady Trumper? Wasn't that very risky?"

Appleby shook his head. "It was a bad business, certainly. But fundamentally she wasn't greatly moved. Again it's a matter of the hidden places of the heart. Deep down, she had known she was only trafficking with a dream."

I was silent for a moment. "And the moral?" I asked.

"It's a Latin one. *Ut pictura poesis.* Paintings and poems are much alike. You can tell lies in either."

THE INSPECTOR FEELS THE DRAUGHT

THE INSPECTOR FEELS THE DRAUGHT

APPLEBY JUMPED out of his car and made a dash for the porch of Branfoot's house. It was pouring cats and dogs. He pushed open the outer door without ceremony. And, as he was a very old friend of Branfoot's, he would have done the same, in these dripping circumstances, with the inner door too. But the inner door was locked. So Appleby rang the bell.

The inner door was opened almost at once—and by the new Mrs. Branfoot in person. Appleby scarcely knew her, so his first words were formal. But she brushed this aside. "Hullo," she said cheerfully. "Do come in. Isn't it frightful? Sorry about the lock-and-key business. Security, you know. But I'm getting used to being married to a top scientist."

Appleby wasn't so sure. There was something uncertain beneath this young woman's assumption of confidence. And it was an odd marriage. Tim Branfoot was his wife's senior by donkey's years; he had been Appleby's tutor in the mid 'twenties. Nor had he been growing less eccentric in the intervening period. The lady might well have her worries.

That Janet Branfoot was at least touchy appeared within seconds. Out of old habit, Appleby had slipped off his coat, taken a step across the hall, and had just begun to push open the cloak-room door. But his hostess pulled him up. "Give it to me, please, Sir John!"

It had been an awkward flash of asperity, and Appleby cursed himself for a tactless ass. Whether metaphorically or actually, a bride doesn't care to have her husband's cronies hanging up their hats unasked. So he handed both hat and coat to Mrs. Branfoot— and she was charming again in an instant. "They're so horridly wet, you see. We'll put them in front of the fire."

The front door opened straight into the hall which the Branfoots used as a living-room. At one end there was an enormous table littered with Tim's calculations and diagrams. At the other end stood a grand piano imported by Janet—and Appleby wondered whether she thumped at it while her husband tried to get his equations right. In between, there was a big circle of chairs and sofas round the fireplace. Janet led the way to this. "Martini?" she asked briskly.

"Yes, please—if I'm not a nuisance. Tim's about?"

"Tim's about, all right—although he's probably asleep. He always does this give-the-brain-a-nap turn at this time, and isn't usually down for another half-hour. But I'll give him a shout." Janet strode to the foot of the staircase and gave a very loud shout indeed. "Tim, here's Sir John Appleby!" She came back to the fireplace. "On Thursdays we give the maids a half-day together."

Appleby wondered if that was how Tim regarded it.

Presently Branfoot appeared. He was probably delighted to see his old pupil, but he signalized the fact only by being extra crotchety. Appleby wondered whether Janet owned a large hidden veneration for scientific genius. Otherwise he couldn't quite see why she had married him.

"You'll stay to dinner," he said. "We don't compete with the Ritz. But no doubt there will be something."

"Yes, do," Janet said. "Soup and then something cold. I'm afraid. Because of both the maids being off."

"I can't see the sense of sending the two sluts off together." Branfoot spoke pettishly over a large gin.

"You know, Tim, that if they go singly, one or other of us has to meet them in the village with the car."

"Fiddlesticks. You could search your Sunday papers for a month without finding a sex maniac dire enough to make a pass at those two." Tim heaved himself to his feet. "But at least I'm getting on, thank God."

Appleby managed to ignore the large discontent evinced in this turn of phrase. "Work going well?" he asked.

"Come and look," Branfoot, led the way to the great table. "Not that you'll understand a line of it. You've wasted your life, John—clean wasted it. With hard work, you'd have been as competent a second-flight scientist as this country holds. Not, of course, that it's much of a country. Been going to the dogs for thirty years or more." Branfoot suddenly halted, stared at his table, and gave a shout of rage. "Janet, blast you, you've been mucking about again!"

"I've certainly been doing nothing of the sort."

But Branfoot flung up his arms. "Here am I, working under pressure—intolerable pressure—and I can't trust my own house-hold not to mess about my papers. It's damnable!"

In no time there was a row. Appleby could do nothing but sit tight and listen. And presently Tim Branfoot's suspicions shifted and deepened. If it wasn't his wife who had been interfering with his papers it was spies. There was stuff here that spies could demand a fortune for. He had suspected something of the sort for a long time. Spies were getting into the house—probably during his naps. And he was going to hunt through the place now.

Appleby wasn't sure how much of this was plumb crazy; he had a notion that Branfoot's material would at least have a high value in the world where scientific research touches industry. So he suspended judgment. And it soon became apparent that Branfoot's house was one in which very considerable precautions were in force. The windows and doors were all as near burglar-proof as could be. Or so it appeared until the search reached the cloakroom.

It was Appleby himself who pushed open the door of this. It was no more than a large cupboard, some six feet by six. Its only other aperture was a metal casement window. And this was wide open.

"There you are?" Branfoot was in a high state of excitement. "That's how the scoundrel's come and gone!"

"Oh dear, oh dear!" Janet seemed abashed. "I still don't believe it—about anything having been spied on or stolen, I mean. But it's my fault about the window. I opened it this morning, because the place seemed stuffy. And I clean forgot to close it again."

The man eventually arrested—it was after Appleby had caused the Branfoots' house to be kept under observation for some weeks—was a photographer called Hatch. He proved to be driving an enormously profitable trade in reproductions of Tim Branfoot's work. Appleby never had any conversation with him. But he did have some talk with Janet Branfoot. It was just before she was arrested, too.

"You see," he said. "if your story was true, that cloakroom window had been open all day. But I knew very well that it hadn't been."

She gave him a hard stare. "You'd noticed it as you drove up?"

"No—not that. The window was invisible round a corner of the house. But I knew, all the same—and within seconds of entering the hall. You remember I was just opening the cloakroom door to hang up my coat, when you stopped me. Again I hadn't an opportunity to *see* anything. But I *felt* something at once."

Janet's face held no expression. "Explain," she said.

"It's quite simple. If a door opens inwards on a very small room, and there isn't an open window or ventilator for the air to escape by, there's a perceptible pneumatic resistance to overcome when one gives a first push. So what happened is clear. When I rang the bell, Hatch was just preparing to leave after one of your joint snooping and photographing sessions while your maids were out and your husband having his nap. So you shoved Hatch into the cloakroom—and of course had then to keep me out of it."

"When I was safely in the house, Hatch opened the cloakroom window and escaped that way. But of course he couldn't close it properly behind him. When I pushed the cloakroom door a second time—during Tim's search of the house, that is—I was conscious at once of the different feel of it. It wasn't under pressure at all."

Appleby paused. "You married your top scientist in haste, it may be said, on the strength of a bright criminal idea. I think it, very likely that you'll be given the opportunity to repent at leisure."

PELLY AND CULLIS

PELLY AND CULLIS

A ND IS that the verdict of you all?"
This second question will sometimes take the foreman of a jury by surprise. But on the present occasion the foreman was an instructed person, who knew he would be required to answer it. He was, in fact, an eminent physician in the town, who on the score of other and more important services to the community could have gained exemption from this chore in court had he chosen to do so. Nevertheless—and perhaps as believing that in a criminal trial one or two trained minds on the jury cannot be amiss—here he was.

The question addressed to Dr. Girdlestone could clearly be answered with a single word—hard upon which the jurymen could go home and dine, comfortable in the feeling that their wisdom had ensured the due punishment of the unrighteous. Dr. Girdlestone, however, resolved upon using two: this from a feeling that "It is," being slightly more emphatic—even weightier—than plain "Yes," better became the gravity of the situation.

"It—" Dr. Girdlestone began.

But the clerk of the court had elevated his right hand the few inches that were required to apprise so alert a man as Dr. Girdlestone that silence was requested of him. The clerk of the court did this because the judge had raised *his* hand and misdoubtingly touched his little wig with his index finger. The clerk had been quite unable to see this gesture, since he could bring the judge into view only by standing up and turning round. But tradition having long constrained him to this disabling situation, he had developed a species of clairvoyant faculty which made him aware of even the smallest movement on the bench. And now the judge spoke.

"Dr. Girdlestone, you must forgive me interrupting you." The judge was much too grand to pretend not to be acquainted with

147

Girdlestone, whom he frequently met at dinner when a Crown Court was being holden in the city. He was also the last man—or woman—of all those present who would deviate for a moment from that inflexible courtesy to the accompaniment of which the English legal profession goes on its prosperous way amid the wiles of criminals and the agitations of litigants. "I am very conscious," the judge went on (and he seemed now to be benevolently addressing the jury at large), "of the strains and fatigues to which you have been exposed while assisting me today. And you may justly feel that a stage has been reached at which the most exigent attention is no longer required of you. Nevertheless, it seems to me desirable that when a question explicitly involving all of you is propounded, all of you should be cognizant of the answer that your foreman gives to the court. So would somebody be so very good as to awaken the gentleman who appears to have fallen asleep in the middle of the front row? It will be no great unkindness, since a jury-box is scarcely well-adapted to comfortable slumber."

There was laughter in court—subdued perhaps out of some decent feeling for the man in the dock. Counsel for the prosecution and counsel for the defence (who had not only been in the Harrow Eleven together but had actually been its opening pair on a number of auspicious occasions) exchanged humorous glances indicative of a common consciousness that old Herriman up there, although getting on for eighty, could still be trusted to keep his form. Meanwhile, somebody had given the peccant juryman a nudge; had given him, indeed, first a gentle and misdoubting nudge, and then another a good deal more vigorous than that. Dr. Girdlestone, still on his feet, observed this performance with composure. But it must have been with a sharp-eyed composure, for suddenly he had uttered the words "If I may have your leave, my lord," and was edging his way along the line of jurors. He stooped over the slumped and immobile figure upon whom all eyes were now fixed. And it seemed a long time before he straightened up again and spoke.

"My lord," he said, "I am a doctor, as you know. In my opinion this man is not asleep, and so cannot be awakened. And it is desirable that help be called and that he be removed from court at once."

"Let that be done. Dr. Girdlestone, I am most grateful to you."

Without more words, Mr. Justice Herriman rose and bowed. The barristers in court rose and bowed. Sundry other persons felt they ought to do this too, but were a little hesitant and slow about it—whereupon they were bellowed at by some functionary to be upstanding in court. But by the time this was achieved Mr. Justice Herriman had gathered his skirts about him and vanished from the bench.

The two Q.C.s and their respective juniors were in a little clump as Sir John Appleby approached. Appleby had been in court because he was concerned in a case that hadn't been called; he had lingered because the present one interested him; these men had spotted him and caused him to be handed a hospitable message. What had happened in the jury-box appeared to have put them in good spirits quite as much as the glass of sherry they were now discussing.

"Odd situation," the first Harrovian said. "If the chap's dead, that is. Take a little thinking out on Herriman's part. Not that he won't have us across there again in no time. He's uncommonly expeditious, as that generation of judges goes. But much too downy an old bird to say anything off the cuff when a thing like that crops up."

"Perhaps he's on the blower," one of the juniors said, "to the Lord Chancellor."

"My dear lad, would you go to a Lord Chancellor for law? Don't make me laugh."

"Or the L.C.J.," the other junior said.

"More likely to be to some fly old crony of his own—who has never strayed out of chambers in his life, but has a useful knack of remembering this and that."

"Is it so complicated?" Appleby asked. "Suppose the man is dead. Isn't it just a question of whether he died before, or after, the verdict was delivered?"

"He certainly didn't die in the jury-room," the second Harrovian said. "He must have walked, or at least tottered, back into court. And it's arguable that, up to this very moment, the verdict has *not* been delivered. After 'Guilty', you know, comes that 'Verdict of you all'. Both questions must receive an answer audible to the whole court."

"What if the judge himself were fast asleep," the first junior asked, "and then woke up and went ahead as if he'd heard what he certainly had not?"

"What, indeed?" The second junior consulted his glass. "But nowadays there's all this business—isn't there?—about when one *is* dead. They may bury that chap in a couple of days time. But I'll bet you a bottle of claret you'd never get that superior sawbones Girdlestone to give a positive opinion as to whether he was alive or dead when they carried him out of court."

"Mere wandering and maundering, this," the first Harrovian said severely. "Unless the man can be brought back into court alive, and be demonstrably alive when the verdict is formally completed and accepted by the judge, there does seem to be an odd little point of law to be considered."

"And there might have to be a retrial?" Appleby asked. "What about a majority verdict? That's allowed at the discretion of the judge nowadays."

"Perfectly correct, Appleby. Eleven good men and true saying 'Guilty'. And one saying nothing at all, because he's dead. It would be like one of those comical cases you used to read in *Punch*."

As he made this remark, counsel for the prosecution glanced over Appleby's shoulder, and his expression at once registered mild dismay. Counsel for the defence followed his glance—and promptly evinced the same perceptible perturbation. Whereupon the two juniors, becoming aware of the occasion of this, seemed on the verge of giving way to panic. Yet all that had happened was the approach of Dr. Girdlestone.

"Good morning," counsel for the prosecution said smoothly. "But I wonder, my dear sir, whether we ought to permit ourselves the pleasure of your conversation? This vexatious case is not closed, and as a result you have not yet been discharged from your position as a juryman."

"Rubbish," Dr. Girdlestone said brusquely.

"Come, sir," counsel for the defence expostulated, coming to the support of his learned colleague. "You must be aware that, absurd though it may be, it is held to be an awkward thing should jurymen be found in talk with officers of the court—which is what barristers and solicitors have the honour to be. So let me suggest that my colleagues and I withdraw. We can leave you in the company of Sir John, of course, who hasn't the slightest connection with the case."

"Then I hope he will have."

"I fail to understand you, Dr. Girdlestone."

"What I mean to say is, that this affair appears to have turned into just his sort of thing. And I think we can forget that punctilio about jurymen having to be treated like lepers, sir. Neither the judge nor anybody else is likely to make a point of it. In view, that is to say, of what has now happened. That unfortunate man is indeed dead. Precisely when he died, I should not care to say." Dr. Girdlestone paused for a moment and frowned, having unfortunately detected a wink passing between the two junior barristers. "But dead he is."

"These sudden things are always rather shocking," counsel for the prosecution said, easily but with proper sobriety. "A heart attack, was it? Or one of those treacherous cerebral embolisms?"

"Nothing of the kind, sir. Decidedly nothing of the kind."

"Then just what did he die of?"

"I have very little idea. Doubtless the pathologists will inform the world in due season. But if you are content for the moment with a very rough answer, I believe I can afford it you."

"And it is?"

"Strong poison. *Very* strong poison. Just that."

An acquaintance of Appleby's, Colonel Hargreaves, had been nominated as High Sheriff of the County in the previous

November, and was still treating his duties very seriously. "I'm afraid I'm rather tied up at the assizes," he would say—a shade anachronistically—in answer to friends inviting him to play golf or shoot pigeons. And on the present occasion he had seen to it that the reading of the judge's commission had been a properly ceremonious affair, and then settled in at a respectable distance on the bench to see the Queen's justice dispensed. And now, since the late mysterious event had taken place within the precinct of the court, he felt that he had a part to play (perhaps in a manner equally mysterious) in its unravelment. This persuasion annoyed the police inspector who had turned up to discover what the fuss was about. He understood about judges, and was prepared to be properly deferential to them on the wholesome basis of having had much opportunity of watching them at work on criminal cases. But a High Sheriff he clearly regarded as a piece of medieval flummery having no title to waste his time. There was, of course, the vexatious fact that Colonel Hargreaves's elder brother, Lord Lumbercraft, was the chairman of the County Council, and therefore in an absurd and remote sense Inspector Roach's employer. But this didn't make Inspector Roach any more pleased with Colonel Hargreaves's fussing around. And it was thus that the retired John Appleby, merely because his name happened to be legendary among the police forces of the land, came to be drawn into a composing role during the perplexed affair that centred upon the trial and conviction—only was it to *be* a conviction?—of Pelly. Pelly was the little rat of a man (although, indeed, a certain physical strength had to be posited of him) who had killed the girl—or who had done so if the prosecution was to be believed. Pelly, it was maintained, had failed to leave ill alone. He had killed the girl after ineffectively attempting to rape her. It was a story nobody had particularly liked listening to.

"I suppose," Hargreaves asked Appleby, "this disgusting Pelly is for the nick for keeps—without, I mean, the nonsense of a second trial and all that?"

"It's hard to say."

"Dash it all, Appleby, anything of the kind would be the most empty formalism! Nothing but a confounded waste of public money and the time of busy people."

"At the moment, one can't be quite sure."

"Dash it all, he did it, didn't he?"

"The jury said so. Or half-said so, and was about to say so fully."

"Good God, man—it's the most utter rot! Do you believe some pal of this filthy Pelly was imbecile enough to think he could muck up the whole case by poisoning a juror?"

"It's conceivable—except for the use of poison. Pelly's devoted friend—if he had one, but why should he?—would be more likely to do a tip-and-run murder in the street, or a quick job with a gun in this very building."

"Aren't jurymen guarded better than that?"

"No, they are not. Or only when it's some sort of showpiece that's going ahead."

"Have they found out anything about this poor bastard Cullis yet?"

"Not much, I gather." The man to whom Colonel Hargreaves had thus disparagingly referred was the unfortunate poisoned juror. "He must have been a householder, or on some electoral role or the like. Roach is after all that now."

"I didn't think that fellow Roach was any too civil."

"No more he was, Hargreaves. But the fact's irrelevant. He struck me as quite a competent man. And here he is."

Inspector Roach was a burly officer, who would clearly have done a good job helping to shove one crowd of senseless demonstrators out of reach of another. Colonel Hargreaves was disposed—most unwarrantably—to treat him as one who was probably out of his depth in this affair. And he scarcely waited until the Inspector had put his flat cap down on a table.

"Well," he barked, "anything to report?"

"Not a great deal, so far." Roach, although entirely clear that he had no duty whatever to report to Hargreaves, only some disposition to confer with Appleby, was impassively polite.

"Story all over the place yet?"

"I think not. Of course there were two or three newspapermen in court. But all they know is that the trial was adjourned when a juror was taken ill. They may be inquiring at the hospital. But it needn't be until the judge returns to the bench tomorrow morning that the manner of Cullis's death becomes public property. By that time, incidentally, the judge will have decided how to proceed."

"No doubt. Meanwhile, what have you discovered about Cullis?"

"A certain amount—and without much difficulty. It turned out that Dr. Girdlestone knew him."

"Knew his fellow juror?" It was Appleby who asked this question, apparently in some surprise. "Girdlestone didn't give that impression when he was coping with the moribund Cullis in the jury-box."

"I think it was simply that it came to him afterwards that he knew the fellow. But only slightly, and by sight. Cullis was a porter at the hospital."

"One of the crowd that runs the place—eh?" Hargreaves asked drily. "A law unto themselves. Have even the consultants right under their thumb."

"Possibly so, sir." Roach seemed to indicate that this sort of disorder in society was one with which, happily, he was not called upon to deal. "A quiet little man, Cullis seems to have been. Married, but no children. We went to his house, of course, and broke the thing to his wife. I did that myself."

"Ah!" Hargreaves got a certain quality of respect into this ejaculation, as if one had to give it to a man whose duty imposed that sort of task on him. "Did she know anything about Pelly?"

"Nothing at all—except that he was being tried today, and what he was being tried for."

"These sort of people," Hargreaves said, "read the local newspapers, which always tell you more or less what is coming along in the courts. So Cullis knew what he was in for."

"Did Mrs. Cullis," Appleby asked, "afford the slightest suggestion that what had happened was something she feared might happen?"

"No, she didn't, Sir John—and of course it's a point one always looks out for." Roach hesitated. "There was something there, all the same."

"In this woman?"

"Well, yes—and in the whole house as well. I found myself just not liking the place. But that's not a helpful thing to report."

"One never knows, Inspector. But stick to the woman for a moment. Was she frightened about something?"

"Yes."

"It wasn't just a matter of her being scared by the sudden appearance of a police officer in uniform—even before you gave her the news of her husband's sudden death?"

"No. One always has to allow for that—even among educated and what you might call sophisticated folk."

"Perfectly true. So what was it?"

"Well, there are people who have to live in dread of they don't at all know what—which must be a good deal worse than being in dread of what you can put a precise name to. And then something bad happens, and they still can't quite relate it to this nebulous anxiety with any precision." Having delivered himself of this, Inspector Roach picked up his cap again. "And now," he said briskly, "I'm going to see if the pathology people have any preliminary finding. It does sometimes happen they just have to take a sniff and they're there in one. And precisely what killed the poor beggar is certainly the next information we want."

With this, Inspector Roach took his leave. And Colonel Hargreaves shook his head dubiously.

"Viewy fellow, wouldn't you say, Appleby? All that about nebulous anxiety, and so forth. Nebulous itself, if you ask me."

"It may sound a bit like that. However, I've no doubt that what you might call the routine inquiries are going on pretty vigorously at the same time."

"Such as?"

"Just what happened in that jury-room. Who had access to it, and when. Do you know, Hargreaves? It sounds rather like the title of a detective story. *The Case with Eleven Solutions.* Something like that."

"I never read the things." The High Sheriff chuckled suddenly. "But I see what you mean. One dead juror, and eleven who might have done the job."

"But, of course, it doesn't exhaust the possibilities. For instance, why not twelve? What about the woman who brought in the tea?"

"The tea? Would there have been tea?"

"Elevenses, Hargreaves. It's a prescriptive thing. Or it might have been a man, you know. Twelve cups of tea, and in one of them the fatal pinch. And he'd see that the one with the pinch got to the right person."

"Good heavens, my dear Appleby—what a horrible idea!"

"Or, of course, it mightn't matter *who* got it. *Any* juror would do. Because with one dead the whole trial would have to be put off till the next sessions. And that would give time for this or that to happen."

"My dear fellow, you can't believe—"

"Well, no—I'm afraid I can't." Most improperly in face of the heinous crime under discussion, Appleby appeared amused by his own extravagance. "But there's something to be said for a play of imagination, you know. It turns up sober truth from time to time."

Appleby was not due home until the next day. So he dined with Burland, the prosecuting Harrovian.

"Would you have been inclined," he asked, "to call that an open-and-shut affair?"

"No."

"You put on a fairly good show of seeming to see it that way."

"My dear Appleby, I was simply carrying out my duty of assisting the court. It's how our odd forensic system works, isn't it? And it was up to Nicky Boxer to do his damnedest t'other way on." Nicky Boxer was the second Harrovian. "And Nicky didn't do a bad job, did he? He made a lot of capital out of all this current talk about the hazardousness of accepting evidence of identity too readily. Pelly, by the way, has a shocking record, which would have been heard about once that verdict was on the books. And he looks it, wouldn't you say? Even so, I thought he had a chance of getting off. Only unidentified fingerprints on that weapon, for instance—and no jury is happy about pukka fingerprints, these days. Comes of reading crime stories. Then again, it was a deed of darkness in every sense. The blanket of the dark—as Shakespeare says—fairly smothering the whole thing. I tell you, Appleby, I was surprised at getting a verdict."

"Do you think Herriman was surprised?"

"It would take a lot to surprise *him*. And, of course, he may have known a thing or two about friend Pelly already."

"Quite so. And of course, Burland, there is no difficulty about a motive in a case like that. We're all supposed to be rapists at heart. And in the wake of rape—or a shot at it—murder is the most natural thing in the world."

"It's a persuasive conventional view. And I agree we weren't put to a stand in the matter of motive. But when we come to the death of this little chap Cullis it's a different matter. We know nothing about him, of course—and all sorts of people may have wanted to kill him for all sorts of reasons. But why do the deed in these very odd circumstances?"

"But we don't know when it was done, do we? It's a matter for the toxicologists. If something comparatively slow-acting was involved, it may have been dropped into Cullis's tea at breakfast by his wife."

"Perfectly true, Appleby—and these small marital disharmonies do occur. But I favour what might be called a more structured view of the thing. Have you thought about Girdlestone?"

"Why should I think about Girdlestone?" This question came from Appleby with perhaps too much innocence. Indeed, it wasn't likely that he hadn't been thinking of Girdlestone, since the physician was the only one of those eleven jurors he knew anything about, so far.

"I hear that a link has been established between him and the unfortunate Cullis."

"That's really a slightly coloured way to put it, Burland. Girdlestone merely recalled, it seems, that Cullis was a porter in the hospital where he, Girdlestone, is a consultant. Girdlestone, in fact, had simply noticed Cullis as in more or less humble employment about the place. That's not much of a link."

"At least it gives scope to imagine one. Suppose, Appleby, that Cullis had been snooping around, and had come upon something discreditable to this eminent leech—"

"A pretty stiff supposition, that."

"Never mind! Entertain it for the moment; infer that Girdlestone decided Cullis must be silenced; reflect that nobody was in a better position than Girldlestone to obtain, and understand how to employ, this poison or that; add the fact that their both having to turn up for jury service afforded an opportunity for close contact such as wouldn't normally be easy to achieve between a top physician and a porter: consider all this, my dear fellow, and the handcuffs ought positively to be jingling in your pocket. By jove—nine o'clock! But shall we have another glass of port?" Burland laughed robustly. "Keeping a sharp eye, of course, on the fellow as he pours it out."

Not much later that evening, Appleby, despite the second glass of port, might have been judged to have developed a surprising thirst. He prowled the city—or the quarter of it in which the hospital lay—on the most pertinacious-seeming of pub crawls. Conceivably because such behaviour was highly indecorous on the part of a former Commissioner of Metropolitan Police, Appleby in fact wasn't looking like anything of the kind. One of the great detectives of fiction, disguised as a flower-girl or a leering Chinaman, might have felt himself first cousin to this commercial gentleman not doing too well in the world. He was such a one, however, who had resisted turning morose or depressed. In fact he was of the chatty sort which attaches itself to the fringes of a companionable group, and listens patiently until allowed to put in a word or two, or perhaps a question or two, of his own.

This was freakish behaviour on Appleby's part, and essentially of a nostalgic order. Hadn't he, as a young man, often frequented pubs in a false nose and spectacles? Well, perhaps not. But certainly similar unassuming labours in the interest of law and order had been his daily, or nightly, round a long time ago. He was rather pleased at this reassumption of an ancient role.

It was simply a question of finding the right hostelry. The unfortunate Cullis's place of employment (and, indeed, Dr. Girdlestone's) was a major teaching hospital with a large staff. Those housemen who were briefly off duty would alone fill more than one public bar. But housemen were no use to him, any more than registrars or nurses or grandees like Girdlestone—or, for that matter, the swarms of minor administrative persons to be found in such places nowadays. What he was after, he told himself brutally, were the chaps who trundle you around, living or dead, on trolleys.

Eventually he ran them to earth, appropriately enough, in a small pot-house called The Jolly Waggoner. Here, without a doubt, were three or four of Cullis's colleagues, already aware of the fate that had overtaken him—or at least aware of his sudden death—and disposed to discuss him in an obituary manner. It was on this colloquy that Appleby successfully edged in.

"In the midst of life we are in death," Appleby said—with the air of one who, in modest degree, would elevate a conversation in the direction of philosophic generality. "It's those sudden calls that tell you the truth of that. Would you have said, now, that his health was bad? You're all in a position to be good judges of that, I'd suppose."

The men addressed stared at Appleby for a moment in a hostile fashion, but then decided to take in good part this promotion to a species of status within the medical profession.

"Nothing wrong with Cullis," one of them said. "Or not from the neck down."

"Close," another said.

"Close and jumpy," said a third. "Chapel-going and that. You'd expect a hymn to be coming from him far more likely than a song— let alone an honest curse. There was something in his eye, though. Not a doubt of that. Like as if he'd slipped the collection in his pocket from under the preacher's nose, and was feeling none too happy about it."

"Is that so?" Appleby said. "Now, that's a remarkable thing."

"It was more remarkable than that," the first man said. "It was as if he was afraid he'd be doing it again tomorrow. A kind of guilty chap, you might say, Cullis was."

"And I can tell you something," the second man said. He had lowered his voice and was glancing circumspectly around him. "Although it's to say ill of the dead, in a manner of speaking. It came out of his coat-pocket in the locker-room. He picked it up fast enough—and with what you might call a snarl at me who was standing beside him. But there it was, open on the floor, and I see'd it there."

"You don't say that!" the first man said.

"That I do. And he ought to have been past the age for such things, to my way of thinking. Mind you, any man may take a quick look inside one at a book-stall, or some such place. That's only human nature, after all. But Cullis had paid money for the book, and that's another matter. It was a hot one, too. The pictures, you know. Photographs they'd taken of people actually doing them dirty acts. Whips and the like—but that just to tickle your appetite for other turns to come. Of course I only got a glimpse of it. But enough's enough. You know the sort of thing."

There was a silence, nobody being disposed to deny that he knew the sort of thing.

"I hope," Appleby said solemnly, "that this Cullis wasn't a married man."

"But that he was. No kids, though—which you might call a merciful dispensation. And do you know what I sometimes wondered?" The second man lowered his voice yet further. "It was whether Cullis had it in him to put a bun in the bloody oven."

Appleby's call on Mrs. Cullis was very brief, perhaps because he had abruptly ceased to enjoy the part he was playing. He was tactful, and he asked no questions of a sort that might have been prompted by the conversation he had taken part in at The Jolly Waggoner. He asked, in fact, only one question that was at all out of the way. And when he got back to his hotel he contacted Inspector Roach on the telephone.

"Tell those chaps in their lab," he said, "not to neglect Cullis's left hand."

On the following afternoon Appleby travelled back to London in the company of Burland.

"You know," Burland said, "I was beginning to take quite seriously that notion of mine that it had been Girdlestone. It would have been deuced odd—but nothing like as odd as what you have pulled out of the hat. The coincidence is amazing, for a start."

"It certainly amazed Cullis. Or astonied him, to use an older and stronger word. There he was, suddenly summoned for jury service in a case in which it ought to have been he who was in the dock. And he wasn't exactly a hardened criminal with an untroubled mind. He was a wretch periodically driven by some insane compulsion to actions which he knew to be hideously evil. It's far from surprising that he possessed himself of that lethal stuff."

"It's surprising that he had access to it—and knew what was what."

"He'd prowled that hospital with his eyes and ears open, no doubt. His original idea must have been to possess himself of the means to suicide if his dealings with that poor girl were found out. But what in the end he couldn't face up to was going scotfree and seeing an innocent man convicted of the crime."

"God, Appleby—was there ever a more blindly selfish death? If he'd even left a signed confession before killing himself—"

"Quite so. We must just suppose that the poor devil had got clear beyond all coherent thought."

"He hadn't got beyond quite a neat job on his own teacup, or whatever it was. By the way, Appleby, I must say you showed a certain power of coherent thought yourself."

"Thank you." Appleby received this gratuitous approbation a shade drily. "It did seem to me that, whether pellet or powder were involved, a human hand must have done the trick with it, and that some trace on the skin might remain to an extent detectable by what is called, I think, micro-analysis. It was in my head when I asked poor Mrs. Cullis whether her husband was right-handed or left-handed."

"I doubt whether it would ever have occurred to the lab boys to have a dekko at Cullis's hands—whether right or left. They'd find the stuff in the tummy, and that would be that."

"My dear Burland, perhaps you underestimate the thoroughness of a well-trained forensic scientist. I simply thought it would be civil to let them know what had come into my head. Incidentally, how are you people going to assist Mr. Justice Herriman to sort things out?"

"There's really no doubt that a verdict against Pelly was brought in. It's a fact it would be hair-splitting to deny. So there will have to be an appeal, and then we'll see all the brouhaha of bringing forward fresh evidence. I shouldn't be surprised if Cullis's fingerprints turn out to correspond with the unidentified ones on that axe, or whatever it was." Burland waved a dismissive hand; the details of the case were already fading from the memory of this eminent Q.C. "It will all be mopped up, of course. But I'm afraid it will be rather a bore."

"At least Pelly will be pleased," Appleby said.

THE MAN WHO COLLECTED SATCHELS

THE MAN WHO COLLECTED SATCHELS

T HE SOCIAL revolution," Warriner said, "has impinged upon our statesmen in varying degree. Jones still sends his boy to Eton. Smith, who is in equally high office, and who sits next to Jones whenever the PM calls a Cabinet, buys *his* boy a brown canvas satchel and sends him to day-school round the corner. This story is about Smith."

"And about Smith's boy?" Elrick asked.

"Certainly. It's about Gervase Smith, who is thirteen."

"No Smith," Byatt said, "whether boy or man, was ever called by so affected a name as Gervase. The idea's absurd."

Warriner smiled. "I'm just *calling* these people Smith," he explained. "It wouldn't be quite proper to give the real name, even in a confidential communication to the club. Particularly as my story displays Smith—Smith Senior, that is—in rather an absurd light."

"But we shall be able to identify him if we hunt round among members of the Cabinet for one who has a son named Gervase?"

"Dear me, no!" Warriner's smile grew momentarily blander. "I've invented Gervase's name too.

"I'm not quite sure where to begin Gervase's story. My own connection with it started when I bumped into him—or he bumped into me—in the street. One of the simple habits of the Smiths' household is that the boy often does his home-work in his father's study. I've sometimes met him there and shaken hands and passed the time of day, when visiting his father on Government business."

Elrick looked rather disturbed at this. "Do we understand"—he asked in his best legal manner—"that this young hopeful sits in upon the affairs of the country?"

"Dear me, no. On an occasion like that, he's politely turfed out, and goes off to his own room. But on our brief meetings he had made quite an impression on me. An efficient child I used to wonder how he had come to inherit such a quality.

"Well, I was walking through Westminster one morning, and taking a short-cut down an obscure side street. There were very few people about, and I noticed Gervase at once—or rather I noticed a schoolboy whom I didn't at first identify I hadn't much chance to do so, because he was walking backwards. I didn't think anything of it. I thought it must be a private game—like stepping from paving-stone to paving-stone in a way that won't bring out the bears. There was a telephone kiosk half-way down the street, and I had just passed it when I came up with the boy. At that moment he took a sideways step—rather as if to get a better view of something in the direction from which he had come—and as I've said, bumped into me. He apologized at once, and then I recognised him.

" 'Hullo, Gervase,' I said, 'and how are you?' "

" '999' Gervase said. Then he appeared to realise that this was a cryptic remark. 'I'm just remembering,' he went on, 'what to dial.' And he pointed to the telephone kiosk.

"I was mildly alarmed. 'Has there been an accident?' I asked.

"Gervase shook his head. 'Not an accident,' he said. 'Some weed's scoffed my bag'."

Byatt paused in reaching for a decanter. "Somebody had made off with the boy's satchel?"

Warriner nodded. "Just that. And it appeared to me that dialing 999 was rather an excessive reaction.

"So I reminded Gervase that it was something one was asked to do only in case of real emergency. It would be better to go to a police-station, or find a copper.

"Gervase then explained that he was keeping the thief under observation. And then, perfectly coherently, he told me his story. He was on his way to school on the top of a bus—which was his custom—when an elderly man sat down beside him and entered into conversation. Gervase regarded this as a situation which should be met with reserve. He therefore, fished out his Kennedy's Latin Grammar and applied himself. But this interested the stranger very much; schoolbooks, he said, were different nowadays, and he would like to compare Gervase's with those he used to have himself. Gervase thought this impertinent. So he put Kennedy back in the bag, strapped it up and said he was very sorry, but he got off at the next stop. At this the stranger leaned across the bus and said something in an excited voice about a fire-engine. Gervase, who is an authority on fire-engines, jumped up to look. And at that the stranger grabbed his satchel and bolted.

"This was a very odd story. But Gervase's account of what immediately followed made it odder still. The stranger dashed down the steps and jumped from the bus, with Gervase in hot pursuit. The bus was going at no more than a crawl and Gervase leaped to the pavement without difficulty. He seemed to have every chance of catching his man. But at that moment a powerful car drew up at the kerb, the man jumped in and it drove rapidly away."

"Gervase Smith," Byatt said, "would appear to have a powerful imagination."

Warriner laughed. "But that's not all. Gervase spotted a cruising taxi, jumped into it, and yelled to the driver; 'Follow that car!' The driver obeyed at once.

"And so Gervase had tracked the thief to a house in the very street in which we were now standing. He had paid the taxi-driver and dismissed him—having read somewhere that cruising taxis are apt to turn treacherous—and when I came upon him he was making his way to that telephone while continuing to keep an eye on the house.

"I didn't at all know how much of the story to believe and I thought the best thing to do was to persuade Gervase to come with me to the door of the house, and ring the bell. He agreed to this—I think he regarded a Foreign Office official as being the next best thing to a policeman—and back we went. I had to ring two or three times before I got any answer. Then the door was opened by a grim-looking elderly woman. But as well as looking grim she looked frightened. So I told his story. And at that the woman asked us in, and then almost at once sank down in tears. Her husband was touched, she said. He had a queer interest in schools and school-boys, and was under some sort of compulsion to collect anything he could lay his hands on that ministered to this obsession. But she knew just where Gervase's satchel would be, and she promised to fetch it at once.

"She was as good as her word. She was back with the thing in five minutes, and Gervase—who had let me do all the talking—sat down to make a solemn inventory of the contents. Everything was there he said. Or everything except his atlas. At this the woman swore the satchel hadn't been opened, and I asked Gervase if he could be quite sure the atlas had been there. He looked at me grimly, and sat tight. He wasn't going to leave he said, until he had his atlas, too. And he muttered something about it being very odd that the old woman was so like Jane."

Warriner paused. "I didn't make much of the muttering, and you will guess what my impulse was, I simply wanted to get away quietly, and have any necessary investigation made later. Gervase had met with something mildly sinister or mad, and would be better out of it. But I now had no disposition to disbelieve any part of his story, and I remembered the bit about the powerful car. It just didn't fit in with our present surroundings which weren't of an order to command that sort of assistance in the pursuit of an obsession.

"So I backed up Gervase. And at that there was a sound at the door, and in came a fellow pointing a revolver at us. It was unexpected, ugly, and perfectly futile. I threw a small marble clock at him; there was a bit of a shindy; and then the coppers came along and collected him. I wonder whether you all see what the whole affair was about?"

There was a good deal of speculation—some of it well within the target area—and then Warriner explained. "Gervase's father had been talking in his study to somebody very important indeed. A map had been required—whether of Europe or Asia, I won't say. Smith Senior had simply grabbed his son's atlas, and the two statesmen had drawn on it certain proposed lines of demarcation of the highest interest to another power. And then Jane came in."

"Jane?" Byatt asked.

"You've heard of Gervase muttering about Jane. She was the Smiths' parlourmaid, and the daughter of the charming couple whom Gervase and I were to encounter. They ran a little family concern in espionage. Well, Jane had brought in drinks, and spotted the business with the atlas. But she wasn't able to contact her papa and mama with the story until the following morning. You'll agree they acted promptly in an effort to secure the information Gervase was carrying round."

THE SHORT STORIES OF MICHAEL INNES

THE FOLLOWING includes all the known short stories published under the name "Michael Innes." For stories collected in this volume, we include details of first publication.

Appleby Talking (London: Gollancz, 1954); United States edition, with the order of the contents changed, entitled *Dead Man's Shoes* (Dodd, Mead, 1954). Contains 23 stories.

"Appleby's First Case"
"Pokerwork"
"The Spendlove Papers"
"The Furies"
"Eye Witness"
"The Bandertree Case"
"The Key"
"The Flight of Patroclus"
"The Clock-Face Case"
"Miss Geach"
"Tragedy of a Handkerchief"
"The Cave of Belarius"
"A Nice Cup of Tea"
"The Sands of Thyme"
"The X-Plan"
"Lesson in Anatomy"
"Imperious Caesar
"The Clancarron Ball"
"A Dog's Life"
"A Derby Horse"
"William the Conqueror"

"Dead Man's Shoes"
"The Lion and the Unicorn"

Appleby Talks Again (London: Gollancz, 1956; New York: Dodd, Mead, 1957). Contains 18 stories.

"A Matter of Goblins"
"Was He Morton?"
"Dangerfield's Diary"
"Grey's Ghost"
"False Colours"
"The Ribbon"
"The Exile"
"Enigma Jones"
"The Heritage Portrait"
"Murder on the 7.`16"
"A Very Odd Case"
"The Four Seasons"
"Here Is the News"
"The Reprisal"
"Bear's Box"
"Tom, Dick and Harry"
"The Lombard Books"
"The Mouse-Trap"

The Appleby File. (London: Gollancz, 1975; New York: Dodd, Mead, 1976). Contains 15 stories.

"The Ascham"
"Poltergeist"
"The Fishermen"
"The Conversation Piece"
"Death By Water"
"A Question of Confidence"
"The Memorial Service"
"Two on a Tower"

"Beggar with Skull"
"The Exploding Battleship"
"The Body in the Glen"
"Death in the Sun"
"Cold Blood"
"The Coy Mistress"
"The Thirteenth Priest Hole"

Appleby Talks About Crime, ed. John Cooper (Norfolk, VA: Crippen & Landru, 2010). Contains an introduction by the editor, an essay by the author about John Appleby, an Afterword by the author's daughter, and 18 stories.

"A Small Peter Pry." *Evening Standard* [hereafter, E.S.], 12 August 1954
"The Author Changes His Style." E. S., 10 April, 1958; *The Saint Detective Magazine* (U.S.), May 1960, as "News Out of Persia"; *The Saint Detective Magazine* (U.K.), July 1960, as "News Out of Persia." [both *Saint* appearances were included with 3 other stories under the collective title "Appleby's Fables"]
"The Perfect Murder." E.S., 5 August 1955
"The Scattergood Emeralds." E.S., 10 August 1954; *Ellery Queen's Mystery Magazine*, May 1955, as "True or False?"
"The Impressionist." E.S., 23 July 1955
"The Secret in the Woodpile." *Ellery Queen's Mystery Magazine*, October 1975; *Ellery Queen's Searches and Seizures* (Dial, 1975)
"The General's Wife Is Blackmailed." E.S., 22 April 1957
"Who Suspects the Postman?" E.S., 9 April 1958; *The Saint Detective Magazine* (U.S.), May 1960, as "In the Bag"; *The Saint Detective Magazine* (U.K.), July 1960, as "In the Bag," [both *Saint* appearances were included with 3 other stories under the collective title "Appleby's Fables"]
"A Change of Face." E.S., 24 April 1957
"The Theft of the Downing Street Letter." E.S., 25 April 1957
"The Tinted Diamonds." E.S., 27 April 1957

"Jerry Does a Good Turn for the Djam." E.S. 7 April 1958

"The Left-Handed Barber." E.S., 23 April 1957

"The Party That Never Got Going." E.S., 19 February 1959

"The Mystery of Paul's 'Posthumous' Portrait." E.S., 8 April 1958

"The Inspector Feels the Draught." E.S., 10 April 1958

"Pelly and Cullis." *Verdict of Thirteen*, introd. Julian Symons (London: Faber & Faber, 1979; New York: Harper & Row, 1979)

"The Man Who Collected Satchels." E.S., 26 April 1957

AFTERWORD

M Y FATHER was benign and equanimous, and he was present at home much more than most fathers. Thanks to academic life in Oxford, hours were spent tapping away with two fingers on his typewriter in his study.

In the study hung two portraits of his ancestors. John Mackintosh, a sandy-whiskered Victorian, had been a physician. He glances to his left, a trifle evasive. Perhaps he finds mildly improper the accompanying portrait of his ancestor Anne Mackintosh. Her character was such that she was known as "Colonel Anne" and her eyes engage with the viewer's—daring for an eighteenth century lady. I was named after her and my father was named after the physician.

Three pieces of graph paper were pinned to the study wall. Each demonstrated the progress of the author in each of three roles. The graph for Michael Innes, detective story writer, rose rapidly; that for J. I. M. Stewart, straight novel writer, rose more slowly; and that for J. I. M. Stewart, academic, for his volume of the *Oxford History of English Literature* (labeled OHEL and referred to feelingly as such) barely rose at all.

In drawers of his desk there were chocolate biscuits and the typescript of a spare Michael Innes—a just-in-case Michael Innes. I enjoyed reading perched high on the library steps. I loved the musty book-pipe smoke-sherry smell of the study. A gas fire kept it cozy in winter, and our black spaniel puppy used to curl up on a foot stool in front of the fire. As he grew Berkeley (named at an undergraduate Sunday tea party after a Bishop Berkeley who'd written a treatise on coal tar) had difficulty curling up tightly enough to remain on the foot stool. Part of him would fall off. With dignity he would rise and re-curl himself. As weeks passed and it got more difficult our hilarity grew. Poor Berkeley. My father loved chocolate. My mother used to find scraps of paper with "thank you dear mistress, signed Berkeley" in her grocery cupboard where precious cooking chocolate had been.

Perhaps my father's longevity was related to the ability to detach himself from his immediate surroundings, the world of his imagination providing an escape from the rigours of life in wartime South Australia and post-war Belfast then Oxford. Travelling across the globe with five children cannot have been easy. My mother was an immensely competent woman. Discipline was her department and my father rarely intervened. When we became truly outrageous, such that "that look" from our mother had no effect, she would catch his eye. Not a word was spoken. He would rise, carry us over his shoulder to our bedroom and close the door.

Only once in my life do I recall being reprimanded by him. I was nineteen and had left school the previous summer. My oldest school friend had spent the previous six months on a VSO (Vocational Service Overseas) assignment on a Pacific island she could canoe around in twenty minutes, and she'd written me a long letter describing life there. With the careless callousness of youth I'd allowed weeks to pass when my father learned I'd not replied to the letter. More in sorrow than in anger, he said, "I fear you suffer from poverty of imagination." The incident left its mark, for I still say to myself, "Huh, I wouldn't have got where I got today if I'd had imagination!" I'm happy to report my friend remained my closest friend.

More typically *castigat riendo mores*. A former pupil recounted how, having read an essay "slight on substance" and purporting to be the labours of an entire vacation, my father's comment was "I think, Bobby, we can consider that an excellent morning's work." Jokes were the meat of our lessons. While holidaying in Holland we had to learn to look left then right before crossing the road, the opposite to our habit in left-driving England. The *Times* newspaper obituary columns having described the demise in a road traffic accident in Holland of some worthy Englishman, my father used to chant:

"Look LEFT look RIGHT, remember Sir Arthur Jay:-
  The chief defect of Arthur Jay
    Was always getting in the way,
  He did it once too often and
    Lies buried in the Netherland."
[Yes, I've changed the name]

In similarly irreverent mode he'd told us solemnly that his cousin Isobel, who'd married a medical missionary in Africa, had been eaten by a hippopotamus. When this couple appeared one day at our front door they were met by a wide-eyed child exclaiming "But you were eaten by a hippopotamus."

An ill-favoured older sister of my mother's, renowned for a cantankerous disposition and severe squint, was not spared. She had married a Mr. Lever whom she'd nursed after the First World War. He died soon afterwards. "Well, well" uttered my father, after one of this lady's temper tantrums, "one can see why poor Lever left'er."

While the propensity to detach himself was entirely comprehensible to a child given to day-dreaming, it could cause irritation to the other car drivers. As a child passenger I'd be aware that from a normal speed the car had slowed to a snail's pace despite the absence of any apparent impediment. Presently a line of cars would hoot and rev engines. When this had no effect we'd be overtaken by cars whose inmates were waving violently at us. My father would courteously acknowledge their gesticulations, no doubt assuming they were people he was supposed to know. Not long ago I heard someone on the radio point out that few poets drive cars. Just as well, I thought, knowing the idiosyncrasies of a prose-writer.

When I recall the irreverent attitude he assumed I smile. For at heart he was a serious man with a deep commitment to his students and his family. His own Edinburgh childhood was marked by long Sunday sermons in the Presbyterian Church with its embedded work ethic. He might enquire at lunchtime whether you'd spent a profitable morning in a jovial tone. You knew the answer should be yes. His own day started well before we awoke. With Trollopian orderliness he would get in a couple of hours typewriter tapping before the domestic daily routine began. He then made breakfast while my mother made the beds, fed the hens, plaited our hair. In those days breakfast was no snatched affair. Porridge or breakfast cereals preceded kippers or bacon and eggs, which were followed by toast with butter and honey or marmalade. Hot milk and coffee. The preparation, for a household of 7 or 8 and at times additional lodgers, required concentration. Perhaps once a fortnight concentration lapsed. "Oh no," I'd hear my mother groan from a bedroom, "he's let the milk boil over again." The evening meal was cooked by my mother for about 7 o'clock. Adjourning then to my mother's drawing room, the normal routine was for each to read their book, companionably, until the 9 o'clock radio news. The news was followed by bed-time and lights were out by 10 o'clock. We were *Morgen Menschen*.

Not long ago I read Anthony Trollope's autobiography and mused how his advice to tyros in chapter XII may have influenced my father eighty years ago. Imagination, observational skill, erudition and industry, pronounced essential for a novelist, my father possessed. However, "that the language should be so pellucid that the meaning should be rendered without an effort of the reader"—ay, there's the rub. The rub that gives rise to the chuckle and causes the reader to reach for a dictionary while reading Michael Innes. His spoken vocabulary could also be mannered. One of our daughters reported indignantly if triumphantly that nobody on her law course had understood her use of the word "animadvert." "It's a word your grandfather uses a lot," explained my husband.

In the summer of 1974 my mother required treatment for breast cancer. In March 1979 the disease progressed. She was nursed with single-minded devotion by my father and died in her own bed, as had been her wish, in May 1979. My parents had enjoyed over fifteen years in their retirement home set in six acres of woodland. Known as Fawler Copse (altered to Fouler Corpse by a wit of a fan) it had an idyllic setting but was isolated. In 1980 my husband and I moved to a larger house in Yorkshire, where we had settled to bring up our four children. As we hoped, my father spent increasing lengths of time with us. His perpetual equanimity provided ballast to the gyrations of a household of young children and his sympathies were always with them:- "I have never felt as proud of a grandchild—" he stated when our four year old daughter resolutely declined baptism alongside an infant sister in the local parish church, and her obstinacy was rendering me, her puerperal mother, apoplectic. "That boy's putting up an impressive fight against the introvert," he pointed out as we parents despaired over school report or orgy-wrecked bedroom.

In September 1986 on his eightieth birthday, at Fawler, surrounded by children, spouses, and a dozen grandchildren, he blew out candles, ate his cake then announced, "I'm coming to live with you now." He disappeared for all of two minutes, returning with one small leather suitcase. "Good," we said and drove the four hours to Yorkshire.

The Russian nineteenth century novelists were the last he enjoyed re-reading. It was sad when we realized the page-marker had ceased its progress and that Parkinson's disease had taken him over.

"Education, education, what's the point of education?" stormed my younger sister. He reflected before replying, "It makes life more tolerable."

Proclaiming himself a rational humanist, though conceding the necessity of a great design to explain the universe, my father died without expectation of an afterlife. To me he remains in a book-lined study smelling of musty books and pipe smoke and sherry. There are chocolate biscuits in a desk drawer; a spare Michael Innes in another; my mother's darning socks on one side of the hearth; Berkeley has given up the footstool and taken over the hearthrug; my sister and I are bathed and be-nightgowned. My father opens a translation of the Odyssey and reads aloud. John Mackintosh is listening, and so is Colonel Anne.

Margaret Mackintosh Harrison

APPLEBY TALKS ABOUT CRIME

Appleby Talks About Crime by Michael Innes, edited by John Cooper and with an afterword by Margaret Mackintosh Harrison, is set in 12-point Palatino by White Lotus Infotech Private Limited. It is printed on 60-pound Natural acid-free paper. The cover illustration is by Gail Cross, and the Lost Classics series design is by Deborah Miller. *Appleby Talks About Crime* was printed and bound by Edwards Brothers, and published in March 2010 by Crippen & Landru Publishers, Norfolk, Virginia.

CRIPPEN & LANDRU, PUBLISHERS

P. O. Box 9315
Norfolk, VA 23505
Web: www.crippenlandru.com
E-mail: info@crippenlandru.com

Since 1994, Crippen & Landru has published more than 90 first editions of short-story collections by important detective and mystery writers.

☞ This is the best edited, most attractively packaged line of mystery books introduced in this decade. The books are equally valuable to collectors and readers. [*Mystery Scene Magazine*]

☞ The specialty publisher with the most star-studded list is Crippen & Landru, which has produced short story collections by some of the biggest names in contemporary crime fiction. [*Ellery Queen's Mystery Magazine*]

☞ God Bless Crippen & Landru. [*The Strand Magazine*]

☞ A monument in the making is appearing year by year from Crippen & Landru, a small press devoted exclusively to publishing the criminous short story. [*Alfred Hitchcock's Mystery Magazine*]

13 TO THE GALLOWS
by John Dickson Carr and Val Gielgud

Never before published! Four plays, two by John Dickson Carr alone and two in collaboration with the BBC's Val Gielgud. *Inspector Silence Takes the Air* is set during World War II at an emergency set of studios in a provincial town. There, a murder takes place—and the weapon disappears. In *Thirteen to the Gallows*, also set in a BBC studio, a woman falls to her death from a tower—it is murder, but no one is near her, and the only clue is a scattering of flowers. *Intruding Shadow* is filled with mysteries within mysteries, as Carr expertly shifts the audience's expectations from one suspect to another. *She Slept Lightly* features the ghostly appearances of a young woman during the Napoleonic Wars.

The introduction and notes are by Tony Medawar.

Numbered clothbound, with add'l pamphlet printing
a previously unpublished Carr radio script, $43.00

Trade Softcover, $20.00

SPEAK OF THE DEVIL
by John Dickson Carr

"On my last public appearance I was hanged by the neck until dead!" An 8-part radio play, broadcast in 1941, featuring duels and chivalry, romance and mystery, and a seemingly impossible crime that turns out to be much too real.

The introduction and notes are by Tony Medawar.

Trade Softcover, $15.00

TRADITIONAL MYSTERIES IN THE LOST CLASSICS SERIES

Crippen & Landru is proud to publish a series of *new* short-story collections by great authors of the past who specialized in traditional mysteries. Each book collects stories from crumbling pages of old pulp, digest, and slick magazines, and most of the stories have been "lost" since their first publication. The following books are in print:

Joseph Commings, *Banner Deadlines: The Impossible Files of Senator Brooks U. Banner*, edited by Robert Adey; memoir by Edward D. Hoch. 2004.

Erle Stanley Gardner, *The Danger Zone and Other Stories*, edited by Bill Pronzini. 2004.

T.S. Stribling, *Dr. Poggioli: Criminologist*, edited by Arthur Vidro. 2004.

Margaret Millar, *The Couple Next Door: Collected Short Mysteries*, edited by Tom Nolan. 2004.

Gladys Mitchell, *Sleuth's Alchemy: Cases of Mrs. Bradley and Others*, edited by Nicholas Fuller. 2005.

Philip S. Warne/Howard W. Macy, *Who Was Guilty? Two Dime Novels*, edited by Marlena E. Bremseth. 2005.

Dennis Lynds writing as Michael Collins, *Slot-Machine Kelly: The Collected Private Eye Cases of the One-Armed Bandit*, introduction by Robert J. Randisi. 2005.

Julian Symons, *The Detections of Francis Quarles*, edited by John Cooper; afterword by Kathleen Symons. 2006.

Rafael Sabatini, *The Evidence of the Sword and Other Mysteries*, edited by Jesse F. Knight. 2006.

Erle Stanley Gardner, *The Casebook of Sidney Zoom*, edited by Bill Pronzini. 2006.

Ellis Peters (Edith Pargeter), *The Trinity Cat and Other Mysteries*, edited by Martin Edwards and Sue Feder. 2006.

Lloyd Biggle, Jr., *The Grandfather Rastin Mysteries*, edited by Kenneth Lloyd Biggle and Donna Biggle Emerson. 2007.

Max Brand, *Masquerade: Ten Crime Stories*, edited by William F. Nolan. 2007.

Mignon G. Eberhart, *Dead Yesterday and Other Mysteries*, edited by Rick Cypert and Kirby McCauley. 2007.

Hugh Pentecost, *The Battles of Jericho*, introduction by S.T. Karnick; afterword by Daniel Phillips. 2008.

Victor Canning, *The Minerva Club, The Department of Patterns, and Others*, edited by John Higgins. 2009.

Anthony Boucher and Denis Green, *The Casebook of Gregory Hood*, edited by Joe R. Christopher. 2009.

Vera Caspary, *The Murder in the Stork Club and Other Mysteries*, edited by A.B. Emrys. 2009.

Philip Wylie, *Ten Thousand Blunt Instruments*, edited by Bill Pronzini. 2009.

Michael Innes, *Appleby Talks About Crime*, edited by John Cooper; afterword by Margaret Mackintosh Harrison. 2010.

FORTHCOMING LOST CLASSICS

Erle Stanley Gardner, *The Exploits of the Patent Leather Kid*, edited by Bill Pronzini.

Vincent Cornier, *Duel of Shadows: The Extraordinary Cases of Barnabas Hildreth*, edited by Mike Ashley.

Phyllis Bentley, *Author in Search of a Character: The Detections of Miss Phipps*, edited by Marvin Lachman.

Elizabeth Ferrars, *The Casebook of Jonas P. Jonas and Others*, edited by John Cooper.

Balduin Groller, *Detective Dagobert: Master Sleuth of Old Vienna*, translated by Thomas Riediker.

SUBSCRIPTIONS

Crippen & Landru offers discounts to individuals and institutions who place Standing Order Subscriptions for its forthcoming publications, either all the Regular Series or all the Lost Classics or (preferably) both. Collectors can thereby guarantee receiving limited editions, and readers won't miss any favorite stories. Standing Order Subscribers receive a specially commissioned story in a deluxe edition as a gift at the end of the year. Please write or e-mail for more details.